Natale Ghent

all the way home

a novel TRANSFERRED TO YRDSB

 Harper*Trophy* Canada™
An imprint of HarperCollins*Publishers*Ltd

All the Way Home
© 2006 by Natale Ghent.
All rights reserved.

Published by HarperTrophyCanada™,
an imprint of HarperCollins Publishers Ltd

Originally published by HarperTrophyCanada™ in a trade paperback
edition: 2006.
This mass market paperback edition: 2009.

HarperTrophyCanada™ is a trademark of HarperCollins Publishers.

HarperCollins books may be purchased for educational, business,
or sales promotional use through our Special Markets Department.

HarperCollins Publishers Ltd
2 Bloor Street East, 20th Floor
Toronto, Ontario, Canada
M4W 1A8

www.harpercollins.ca

Library and Archives Canada Cataloguing in Publication

Ghent, Natale, 1962–
All the way home / Natale Ghent.

ISBN 978-1-55468-413-7

1. Horses--Juvenile fiction. 2. Family--Juvenile fiction. 3. Fathers and
sons--Juvenile fiction. I. Title.

PS8563.H46A75 2009   JC813'.6   C2008-904044-9

HC 9 8 7 6 5 4 3 2 1

Printed and bound in the United States
Set in Dante

For Mum

chapter 1
moving on

They say that a house has a memory, just like a person. That it gathers up all the anger and sorrow and happiness of the lives that have lived inside and holds it, like ghosts in the walls. I even heard once about a woman who moved into a place that was haunted by the laughter of the family that lived there before, and she could hear it when she walked from room to room, which sounds kind of scary.

But I know that a house is just a house, and it's people that do all the remembering. A house is only yours when you're in it, and the only memories that matter are the ones you take with you when you leave the place behind.

I'm thinking about this because we've sold our house and there's no turning back now. The real estate man was all teeth and gladness when Ma signed the papers, sealing the deal. I'm not happy about it, even though I know the money will allow us to keep Smokey. It's only been a few months since that day when, faced with having to sell Smokey, I ran away and the cops chased me home, but somehow it seems like years. Despite every-thing, I managed to graduate, getting straight A's in all my classes. Now summer vacation is here, and I'll actu-ally be going to high school this fall.

Looking back, it probably wasn't the best idea in the world to take off on Smokey, but I just couldn't stand the thought of selling him to some other kid. A pony like Smokey doesn't come along every day, so I was forced to take drastic measures. And if selling our house means we get to keep Smokey then I can live with that. Still, I have to confess I'm worried. Because where we're going isn't a house. It's an apartment.

I've never lived in an apartment before but I can imagine it isn't at all like living in a home that you own. Besides, the only people who live in apartments in Eastview are the ones the newspaper calls "unfortu-nate." I hate thinking about us like that, and I know Ma hates it too. To me, apartments are like train stations. They're just a place to rest your feet on your way to somewhere else. Nobody owns them. Nobody cares if there are flowers in the garden or whose scuff marks are on the floor. If buildings really do have memories, then apartments must have the hardest job of all, try-ing to piece together all the different lives that have travelled through.

Ma is trying to make things easier on us. She says

it will be exciting to live in an apartment, just like millions of people in New York do. But it makes me sad to think of moving. To think about some other kids running up the stairs the way that Cid, Queenie and I did over the years. Sleeping in our bedrooms as though we'd never lived there. Painting over the yellowed walls that I've stared at almost every night for five years, and sometimes during the day when I would lie on my bed thinking. It's not like we haven't moved before. It was hard leaving our other houses too. But at least when we left we knew that we had another home to go to.

I'm trying to put on a happy face so that Ma won't feel any worse than she already does. At least Queenie doesn't seem to mind that we're moving, which is a good thing. It would break Ma's heart to see her upset, she worries about her so. Queenie has a habit of escaping into her own little world when she gets scared or out of sorts. She dances her little dance and thinks her own thoughts to hide from the world. But Queenie is so excited about the fact that we get to keep Smokey that she could care less about where we go. She doesn't even mind that we've had to keep Smokey up at Ted Henry's field until we can afford to move him to someplace better, the way Ma promised. I was dead against keeping Smokey in Ted's field, for obvious reasons, the biggest being that Ted Henry was the last person I wanted to see after I ran away and spoiled his plans to sell Smokey. But we're the only customers he has left after a fire reduced his barn to a pile of charred wood and blackened stones. In any case, Ma arranged the whole thing and said it was best, seeing as we couldn't keep Smokey out back in the shed for months while we waited for the money from the house to come in. She said that everything would be fine now and that she'd even buy us a brand new saddle, which is all Queenie talks about.

Cid's another story, though. She's been holed up like a badger in her room for days, blasting her David Bowie albums. Ever since the house got sold she's been all weird and acting like she doesn't care about any of us any more. She's fifteen now, but that doesn't give her the right to act the way she's been doing. Just last week I saw her hanging around with a group of boys outside the school. They didn't look like they were up to much, and when I called out to her, Cid turned away as though she didn't even know me, her own brother. I bet Ma would love to hear that. And then she threw all Queenie's things into the hallway and she won't even let her sleep in their room. It's not a problem, really. Queenie has been sleeping on the pullout couch with Ma, because their beds are dismantled for the move. My bed is in pieces too, but I'm sleeping on my floor in a sleeping bag. I don't mind. It's kind of like camping.

Still, I can't get over what a jerk Cid is. I made the mistake of knocking on her door and she just about tore my head off, so we're all just leaving her alone, including Ma. I have no idea what she's been doing in her room for the last three days, and quite truthfully, I don't want to know. I thought I smelled smoke through her door at one point.

But aside from dashing like a fugitive into the bathroom once in a while, she's been hunkered down, blaring her music, like she has no intention of moving. At least she's not playing the Bee Gees, knock on wood.

I've already finished packing my room, which was a lot of work. I'd rather be out riding Smokey than dealing with any of this, or just hanging out in the summer sun like every other kid in town. But there's no time for such idleness. Everything has to be packed and ready to go by tomorrow. I'm amazed how much stuff I've collected over the last few years. I tried to throw away as much as possible because Ma said we won't have a lot of room in the new place. I can't bring myself to get rid of some of my things, like my Spider-Man comics and some of my paperback books, so I packed them up in boxes and labelled them with a black Magic Marker. I just hope the new place has a closet or something.

The Salvation Army got most of my clothes, they're so old and worn, so I won't have to pack them. I feel sorry for the poor person who's worse off than me and willing to pay money for those rags. I didn't mind giving them away because Ma says she'll buy me some new stuff. All I really want is a pair of Levi's and some shirts. And maybe a new pair of sneakers. White Adidas would be nice.

Queenie bumps into me as I'm leaving my room to start packing up the basement. Ma asked me to do that once I finished with my own things.

"I need more boxes," she says. She's dragged all her belongings from the hallway to the living room downstairs and has been packing there.

"I just gave you a dozen less than an hour ago," I say. "You can't need more already."

"I do, Nat. The others are full."

This I have to see, because I'm the one who's going to have to trek to the grocery store to get more boxes if we need them. I march down to the living room and look at the work she's done. The boxes stretch end to end across the floor with one blanket-wrapped baby doll or stuffed animal per box, laid out like little cardboard coffins at some kind of weird funeral home.

"Queenie, you have to pack properly." I reach for one of the boxes, folding the flaps down.

"No, Nat!" she says, snatching the box from me. "They'll *suffer-cate* if you close them up."

I have to check myself because I'm feeling really irritated. I should have more patience with Queenie because she's only nine, but between Cid doing nothing, and Queenie using up all the boxes in the house, I'm ready to scream. "Your animals will be fine," I tell her. "They won't suffocate because they're just going up the street to the apartment. It won't take long enough to suffocate anything, not even a real person."

Looking around the room, I notice that she has placed her cast from when she broke her collarbone into a box by itself. The plaster is yellowed and beginning to crack and crumble but you can still make out the stickers and autographs of the people who signed it. I pick it up in disgust. It's starting to smell funny too. "Why do you want to keep this, Queenie? There's no room in the apartment for old junk. Ma said."

Queenie's lips start to quiver like she's going to cry.

"Fine. Keep it," I say, dropping the cast back into its box. "But I'm not going to get more boxes just yet. You're going to have to pack these ones a little better."

I leave her to her mess and go into the kitchen. Ma is there, scrubbing the floor. She has a kerchief tied around her hair and by the way she's working you'd think we were expecting royalty instead of moving. The floor's so clean it gleams. Ma frowns as she works, like she's trying to scrub away her troubles along with the dirt. Seeing her like this, it occurs to me that selling the house just might be the best thing to happen to Ma in a long time. She's been struggling so hard to keep things together since Dad left that it may be a relief to start over with a clean slate.

Ma stops scrubbing and sits back on her heels to rest. She rubs her forehead with her hand as though she has a terrible headache. She's obviously exhausted. When she turns and sees me watching her from the doorway, she smiles and gives a little wave. I wave back, then leave Ma to her work. I know there's still a mountain of junk in the basement to contend with.

I grab a roll of tape and a handful of newspaper from the pile that I brought home from the depot. I quit my paper route for the time being, even though I could use the money. I just don't have time to deliver papers with all this other activity going on. Mr. Smith, the depot man, was pretty nice about it. He said he'll give me another route, no problem, if I decide to come back. My customers were pretty nice too, for the most part. Not Mrs. Geeter—she was always a suspicious old bag, thinking I was up to something. But the rest gave me extra-big tips during my last collection as a way to say thank you for the years of service I've given them.

In the basement, a stack of empty boxes waits for me, and it's a good thing, because there's a whole sea of rubbish that needs to be organized. I don't even know where to begin. Ma's trusting me to sort through the piles and come up with something more "reasonable." There must be a thousand spiders living down here, judging by the webs hanging everywhere. It's a mover's nightmare, with mouldy grocery bags full of old school papers, decaying board games, chipped flowerpots, miscellaneous bicycle parts and battered Christmas ornaments. There are old boots and shoes and coats that none of us have worn in a hundred years, and broken-down boxes of mystery items that no one in their right mind needs that we must have dragged from our other houses. Why do we keep all this garbage?

If nothing else, it's cool down here. The rest of the house is an oven, and it's only June. I open a rickety box at the top of a heap and the first thing I see is a foolscap scrapbook tied with a ribbon. I open it up and there, on the first page, is a picture of the three of us kids, standing in a small plastic wading pool in the backyard of our house in Brookfield, Illinois. The chestnut tree that Cid and I used to love to climb (Queenie was just a baby) is in full bloom to one side. You can see the back alley and the place in the yard where Dad used to make us a skating rink every year. You can even see the tomatoes that Ma planted. We're all smiling in the pool—even

Cid—and we've got washcloths and soap because Ma used to let us bathe outside like that. It makes me feel so strange to see us all happy in another time. It may as well be someone else's life. I flip through the rest of the scrapbook and it's filled with old photos and small poems and assignments that we wrote in school when we were little. Ma kept them all together and arranged them neatly on the pages. It suddenly dawns on me that this particular packing process is going to take a very long time. I place the scrapbook to one side and look to see what else is in the box.

Beneath a bunch of old papers there are three delicate, hand-painted eggs from Easter a long time ago. The eggs are hollow with our names written in yellow crayon on the shell so that the letters stand out against the dye. Cid's is red, mine is blue, and Queenie's is green. The dye has faded but the eggs still have ribbons tied in a bow at the top for hanging them like ornaments, and except for a thin crack along the bottom of mine, they're all intact. Even though I have no idea what we will do with them, I decide to keep the eggs and take a piece of fresh newspaper to wrap them more carefully for their trip to the apartment.

As I'm wrapping the eggs, I notice a headline in the newspaper. Somebody stole Charlie Chaplin's coffin from his grave! I check the date on the newspaper and it says March 2, 1978—three and half months ago. I must have been worrying about Smokey at that time not to notice such a weird story. There is a picture of Mr. Chaplin from one of his movies, and the paper calls him Sir Charles Spencer Chaplin, which sounds pretty high-class for a guy who dressed as a tramp for most of his life. It goes on to say that he was the most famous silent actor in Hollywood. He was born in London and his father left him and his brother in the care of their "unstable" mother. But the father died an alcoholic when Mr. Chaplin was only twelve, and his mother was admitted to the Cane Hill Asylum in England, where she later died.

This makes me feel sorry for Mr. Chaplin. I'm happy that he managed to become famous, in spite of every-thing, although I can't help comparing his life to my own. I think about Ma and wonder if she could become "unstable" too because Dad left us five years ago. I was only eight when he drove off in his silver Pontiac Parisienne, leaving us behind. At first I believed that he would come back. But he never did, and I don't know if he ever will. It's been hard on all of us not having him around, especially Ma. I don't really know what being "unstable" means but I have an idea. I make a mental note to keep a closer eye on Ma, for all our sakes, and then I turn back to the article.

It talks about how Mr. Chaplin died on Christmas Day last year at the age of eighty-eight and says that he was buried in Vevey, Switzerland. But his body was stolen by grave robbers who tried to extort money from the grieving family, which must be the lowest crime in the world. The criminals were captured and their plan foiled—though it took eleven weeks to find the coffin where the grave robbers left it: near Lake Geneva, only ten miles from the cemetery.

A shiver runs up my spine as I imagine Mr. Chaplin's coffin sitting in the woods, just thrown out there where anyone—even bears and wolves—could find it. I stare at his picture a little longer. He looks kind of crazy with his funny eyes and his rumpled suit and round hat. He has a moustache like Adolf Hitler, and I have to wonder: who had the moustache first?

I shake the image of Charlie Chaplin's coffin out of my mind and continue to pack. I only have one box done. The basement will never get finished at this rate. I'm just about to storm upstairs to force Cid to come down and help me when I see something interesting hidden off to one side behind a pile of rubble. It's an old trunk with a small brass padlock, tucked away in one corner where no one would see it unless they knew to look.

Clearing the junk away, I pull the trunk out. I can

tell that it's very old. It's mustier than any of the boxes down here. The leather straps are cracked and falling apart. The padlock is useless, I discover, as the straps just pull away from the trunk when I test them, allowing me to open it from the back. I lift the creaky lid carefully, so as not to break anything, and I look inside.

Just then, Ma calls down from the top of the stairs.

"Everything all right down there?"

I slam the lid shut like I'm guilty of something, even though I have no idea what's in the trunk. The fact that it's padlocked probably means I shouldn't be looking inside. But I'm curious as a cat to know what's in there. I shout up that everything's fine so she won't get suspicious and come down.

"Do you have enough boxes?" she asks.

"I'm okay for now."

"I can go to the grocery if you need more . . ." I hear her step onto the top stair.

"It's okay! . . . I'll go later if I need to."

This seems to satisfy her. I listen to her footsteps as she walks back to the kitchen to continue cleaning. I feel bad for sneaking around, but, like I said, I really want to know what's in the trunk. I don't know why Ma never mentioned it or how it managed to sit down here all these years without my knowing about it. I raise the lid again and look inside.

At the very top there is an old military uniform folded neatly. I can tell right away that it's Dad's from when he was in the Merchant Marines. He was only fifteen when he joined. He wanted to join the real Marines but they wouldn't let him because he was too young, so he signed up with the Merchants instead and worked as a cook. His father didn't want him to go to war but Dad kept running away until his father had no choice but to sign him up. I heard Dad tell that story once—a long time ago—but he wouldn't talk about it when I asked him. I think he was afraid that I would get a similar idea in my head and want to be a soldier too. I knew that he was a wild young man and that he left his father's wheat farm out in Saskatchewan to fight overseas. But I had no idea that he'd kept the uniform. The fabric is deep blue with every button tightly in place, and except for some dust and a few tiny moth holes, you'd never know it'd been stuck in an old trunk for all these years.

I peek inside the lapel to see if there's a name tag or a label and find an old wristwatch and a gold-framed photograph of Dad. He's young and dressed in the uniform and he looks great. There's something funny about the photograph, though. It looks like it's been painted, because Dad's cheeks are really red and the uniform is blue but the rest of the picture looks like an old black-and-white photo. I turn it over to see if there's a date but there isn't. The back is covered in faded brown paper held with the smallest nails I've ever seen. I'm half tempted to pull them from the frame to see if there is anything else inside but I just place the picture carefully on the basement floor and test the watch. I wind the mechanism and it actually works. I adjust the time and put it on my wrist. The brown leather band is still in good shape. The watch feels fine and I like the way it looks so I decide to keep it. When I'm finished admiring the watch, I lift the uniform gently from the trunk. My heart skips a beat when I see what's there and I have to rub my eyes to make sure I'm not imagining things.

I'm not. It's an old rifle.

chapter 2
the big secret

I just about jump out of my skin when Queenie comes clattering down the basement stairs. "What do you want?" I shout as I slam the trunk shut, hiding the rifle. I stand in front, hoping she won't notice it.

Queenie gives me a hurt look. "Why are you yelling at me? You've been yelling at me all day."

I soften my voice and try to act like I don't know there's a rifle in the trunk behind me. "Sorry," I apologize. "I'm just tired from all this packing."

Queenie nods and cranes her neck to see what I'm hiding. "What's in the trunk?"

"Nothing."

"Can I see?"

"Are you through packing your things?" I ask, to throw her off the scent.

"I told you, I need more boxes."

"Did you fill up the other ones?"

Queenie hesitates. "Yes," she says, though she doesn't sound very sure of herself. She's probably been up there dancing instead of packing.

"Did you?" I ask again, the way Ma does if she suspects that we might not be telling the whole truth.

Now it's Queenie's turn to look guilty. I take advantage of the situation, gesturing widely at the room with my arms. "I have to pack all this stuff down here, Queenie. If you need more boxes you'd better ask Ma. She said she was going to the grocery to get more."

"Okay," Queenie says. She gives me a funny look before she turns around and makes her way back up the stairs.

I wait to make sure she is well out of range, then open the trunk again.

The rifle looks really old and it's beautiful. The wood is a rich, reddish brown and it has a big looped metal lever on the bottom. I pick it up and I'm surprised how heavy it is. On the barrel there is a brass plate with the name "Lazy Boy" scratched into it, next to the words "Winchester, 1892." The rifle is almost one hundred years old! There's a little chamber on the right-hand side where the bullets go, I imagine. I check it and it appears to be empty.

I sit there for quite a while just holding the rifle. It's been in the house all these years. It must be Dad's, but there is no way that Ma knows about it. She can't abide guns and would never have allowed one in the house. And I don't blame her. But this isn't just a gun:

it's a piece of history. I raise the rifle as though to shoot, cocking the lever. The action is smooth considering how old it is. I wonder how many hands have held it and how Dad came to own it. Did he use it as a boy on his family's farm? Was he a good shot? It occurs to me that Ma might know about the rifle and the uniform after all. Maybe she just couldn't bring herself to get rid of them because, deep down inside, she still loves Dad. I think about this for some time until I notice something else in the bottom of the trunk. It's a small, cotton drawstring bag.

I place the rifle on the floor next to the uniform and pick up the bag. I'm stunned to find that it has bullets inside. There's no way Ma knows about these. The only explanation for any of this is that she never looked inside the trunk but just put it in the basement and forgot about it. I wonder why Dad left it behind. Maybe he forgot about it too. All I know is that I have to sneak this stuff out of here or Ma will make me get rid of it. It's not that I love guns or anything like that. I just can't allow Ma to give it away before I've had a chance to find out more about it. Besides, all I have to remember Dad is a photo and an old White Owl Cigar box that I keep my money in. If the rifle is his, then I feel I have the right to keep it.

I wrap the rifle in one of the coats hanging in the

basement. Removing the watch from my wrist, I stuff it in my pants pocket. I don't want Ma to see it and start asking questions. The uniform, bag of bullets and the picture I place in a brown paper bag with handles. Then I creep to the bottom of the stairs for surveillance. Ma is talking to Queenie in the kitchen and there's the sound of Cid's music from her room. Trying to be cool, I emerge from the basement carrying the rifle and uniform. I move nonchalantly through the hallway and up the stairs. I've almost reached my bedroom when I hear Queenie coming up behind me. I dash the rest of the way in and slam my door. My room looks like a warehouse with all the boxes and there's nowhere to hide the rifle. I'll have to tuck it in behind a pile of stuff and hope that no one comes snooping around. Queenie, I can handle. But if Ma or Cid sees the rifle, I'm done for. Not that Cid has any particular prejudice against antique rifles. She's just so high-and-mighty all the time, she'd probably jump at the chance to get me in trouble. It's best if I steer clear of her altogether.

After stashing the rifle, I head back to the basement to continue packing. As I pass Cid's room, the music suddenly stops, the door bursts open and Her Royal Highness herself appears. I do a triple take because I can see she's done something crazy. Her hair is short and wild and bleached almost white. Her eyes are ringed with black and she has a giant safety pin with a feather on the end in one ear. To make matters worse, she smells like the whole cosmetics section of a department store, and all I can say is this: "Ma's gonna kill you."

Cid scowls, pops a big pink bubble of gum right in my face and shoves past me in the hall. She trots quickly down the stairs, pulling her jean jacket on as she disappears out the door. I stand at the top of the stairs staring down through the vapour trail of perfume while Queenie gapes up at me in disbelief.

"Was that Cid?" she asks.

For the first time in my life I'm at a loss for words. I think Cid's gone nuts, and I can tell by the look on Queenie's face that she's thinking the same thing. I have no idea what Ma is going to say, but I can tell you she isn't going to be happy. I know Cid is out of sorts by the way she's been moping around and hiding out in her room. Queenie is still standing at the bottom of the stairs like she expects some kind of explanation for Cid's behaviour.

"Do you think she's gone to see Smokey?" she asks at last.

"Not dressed like that," I say. Queenie and I stare at each other until I finally walk down the stairs to continue packing up the basement.

What I really want to do is walk over to see Smokey myself. I don't like the idea of him out in the field unattended for long stretches of time. He gets lonely and I'm afraid that he'll jump the fence, or that some kids might sneak into the field and try to ride him. For some reason, this makes me madder than ever at Cid. How can she be so selfish, leaving the rest of us to do all the work while she runs around with white hair and safety pins in her ears like some kind of punk rocker?

I'm fuming as I survey the mess in the basement. But after an hour or so of packing, I cool off a bit and find my mind drifting back to the rifle. I wonder again at how it managed to sit in that trunk for so many years without anybody knowing about it. I think about the letters scratched into the brass: "Lazy Boy." Why would someone write those words? Who is "Lazy Boy" and why was his name written there? This occupies my thoughts for a very long time, and after hours of packing and thinking, I decide something that I probably shouldn't. I'm going to take the rifle out to the woods and fire it, just to see how it feels and sounds. I know exactly where I can go, too, so that no one will hear or see me and no one will get hurt. I'm really excited by the idea and kind of scared, which probably explains the decision I make next. I'll go tonight, in the dark, after everyone is asleep.

chapter 3
playing with fire

Ma orders pizza for dinner, which is great. She says it's more fun than cooking and easier, considering our whole kitchen is packed up in boxes now. I notice she gives the delivery guy a whole dollar tip. She must be feeling generous, knowing that we won't have so many bills hanging over our heads soon.

"Call Cid for dinner," she says as she carries the pizza into the living room.

"Uh . . . Cid's out," I say, trying to sound casual about it. Cid might be a jerk, but I don't feel like getting her into trouble right now.

"I thought she was up in her room packing," Ma says.

"She went out . . . for some fresh air," I say. It's not a total lie.

"But I ordered mushrooms on the pizza the way she likes." Ma frowns and drops the pizza box carelessly onto the seat of a chair.

This concerns me, because Ma is the first one to tell you that it's a sin to treat food with disrespect. My mind flashes instantly to Charlie Chaplin and his mother. What exactly was it that made his mother unstable? Were there warning signs? I'm sure treating a pizza disrespectfully doesn't mean anything. Ma's just tired out, I guess, or too fed up to care about such things at this moment. Still, it's out of character for Ma to behave this way. I smile extra nicely as she hands us napkins and begins doling out the slices.

"Thanks, Ma!" I say, with a little too much enthusiasm.

Ma takes a slice of pizza for herself, then sits on the floor with her back against the wall. Queenie immediately begins pulling the olives off her pieces. I watch Ma for her reaction but she doesn't seem to mind. If you ask me, it's a waste of good food to discard half the toppings, but I'm not going to say it. Ma's probably happy that Queenie is eating at all, she's so picky. All she ever wants to eat is macaroni and cheese. I put Queenie's discards on my four slices and wolf them down.

"Thanks, Ma," I say again. "That was a really good supper."

Ma looks at me quizzically. "Well, it was only pizza, Nathaniel, but you're welcome."

I surprise us all by giving Ma a little kiss on the cheek before excusing myself to the basement for more packing.

I work until it grows really dark outside. Ma eventually calls down to tell me to quit for the night, but I tell her that I'm okay, I just want to get as much done as possible so we're ready for the movers. I've actually managed to wrangle most of the junk into a reasonable pile. By ten o'clock, Cid isn't home yet and it seems like Ma and Queenie will never go to bed. I think that maybe Ma is waiting for Cid to appear and she must be worried, but then I hear them getting the pullout couch ready. They're talking softly and I can tell they're settling in.

When I'm sure Queenie and Ma are in bed, I go up to my room as though to call it a night as well. So Ma won't get suspicious, I climb into my sleeping bag and wait for the quiet to ease over the house. Lying there, I can't help but wonder where Cid is. I hope she isn't doing anything stupid. I watch the moon rise like a slow searchlight into the bottom corner of my window, bathing the pyramid of boxes in a ghostly glow. As I look around my room, I start to prepare myself to say goodbye. We've been happy in this house, despite everything, and my heart is suddenly heavy with a deep sadness that I didn't even know was hiding there. I turn my mind to Smokey and think of him standing out in the field, a pale, phantom pony in the dark. The sadness loosens its hold on me because I know that there isn't a house in the world that's worth what Smokey is worth to me.

By the time the moon touches the top of my window frame, I decide it's safe to sneak out. I wrap Lazy Boy in an old blanket and carefully push two bullets into my pants pocket. I don't want to bring them all in case I get caught. It would be hard to explain to the police why I was out walking around at night with a rifle and a bag of ammunition. I wouldn't blame them for being suspicious about that.

Cid's still missing in action, so I go into her room to get Smokey's bridle. I creep in and silently close the door. When I flick on the light, I'm surprised to find everything packed and ready to go. So she wasn't just moping around in here. She even took the time to label all her boxes with a black Magic Marker, the same as I did. I guess I owe her an apology.

I grab the bridle and turn out the light, shutting the door slowly so as not to make any noise. Navigating the stairs with my contraband bundle, I'm careful to avoid the steps that will creak and give me away. As I sneak past the doorway to the living room, through the hallway to the TV room and then the kitchen, I can hear Ma and Queenie breathing in the soft rhythm of sleep. I stop to glance at them, nestled on the pullout couch, Queenie's endless little boxes covering the floor.

Ma and Queenie look so comfortable, sleeping together like that.

The door to the mud room gives a little *whoosh* as I pull it open. Feet crammed in my sneakers, my heels hanging over the backs, I scuff my way down the stairs, easing the door closed behind me. I don't want to risk making noise by putting my shoes on in the house so I wait until I'm safely outside. The night is sultry and close with a symphony of crickets chirping loudly. The moon is a giant silver disc hanging in the starry sky. It seems to wink at me as I shuffle through the wet grass, and it's funny, but I could swear I smell the smoke of Dad's cigar.

I lay my bundle down so I can put my shoes on properly. I'm just congratulating myself on my stealth when a voice pierces the quiet and I let out a yelp of fright.

"Where do you think you're going?"

It's Cid, sitting in the dark on the old church pew Ma keeps in the backyard. She crushes something with her foot and I realize that the sweet smell of tobacco was coming from her.

"You were smoking."

She looks at me smugly and doesn't even seem to care that she's been found out.

"What's in the blanket?"

"Nothing."

Cid smiles and shakes her head. "You are such a bad liar, Nathaniel. You'd think you'd be an ace at it by now." She gets up and walks toward the bundle.

I pick it up and consider running, but what good would that do? Cid would call for Ma and I'd be found out and the whole thing would blow up in my face. "I'll make you a deal," I say.

Cid laughs confidently and I know right away that I won't get the better of her this time. What's more, I feel like a stupid little kid standing next to her with all her makeup and her wild hair. She looks really grown-up. "I won't tell Ma you were smoking if you don't tell her about this." I gesture with the bundle.

"I want to know what it is first."

I eye her for a minute. "Okay, fine. But I can't show you here. I'll show you in the park."

"The park? What are you up to, Nathaniel?"

"Just trust me."

Cid follows me obediently to the park. She's so curious about what I'm doing that she doesn't even waste her breath admonishing me. When we reach the cannons, I crouch down in the shadows and Cid does the same. She whistles high and soft when she sees the Winchester.

"Holy crap, Nathaniel, you are in so much trouble. Where did you get this?"

"I found it in the basement—in an old trunk of Dad's."

Cid squints. "How do you know it's Dad's?"

"It was underneath his uniform from when he was in the Marines. There was a watch, too, and a picture of Dad wearing the uniform." I show Cid the watch. She glances at it briefly.

"Is he holding the gun in the picture?" she asks, picking up the rifle and admiring it.

I shake my head. "Maybe he used it on the farm when he was a boy."

"It probably doesn't even work." She checks the action on the lever, the same as I did. And then she turns to look at me.

Our eyes meet, and I can tell by her face that she suddenly understands why I was creeping around in the dark.

"No, Nathaniel! You're not going to do it."

"Just once," I say. "I just want to see what it feels like."

"Ma will kill you if she finds out."

"She doesn't have to find out. You're the only one who knows, so if you don't tell, no one will be the wiser."

Then Cid notices Smokey's bridle over my shoulder.

"I was going to ride him to the meadow in the woods," I confess. "No one will hear the gun there. And there isn't a house for miles, so no one can possibly get hurt."

Cid shakes her head as though she can't believe what

I'm saying. I know now that she isn't going to squeal on me, but I'm not prepared for what she says next.

"I won't tell . . . but you have to agree to one thing. You have to let me shoot first."

"Forget it!" It's just like Cid to take over.

"Fine, then, Nathaniel. Say goodbye to your rifle." She reaches for the Winchester.

"Okay, you can shoot first," I agree, because I'm sure Ma won't care two shakes about Cid smoking once she gets wind of the gun.

"And we take turns riding Smokey," Cid adds.

I'd love to deck her at this point but I have no choice but to concede. "Fine," I say.

★ ★ ★

Cid and I walk across town to Ted Henry's field. I'm carrying the rifle in the blanket and Cid has Smokey's bridle slung over her shoulder, the snaffle bit bouncing lightly against her back as she walks. We don't say much, so I have the opportunity to just let my mind wander. It's funny how things so familiar during the day can seem so strange in the dark. We've walked this road so many times I could do it blindfolded. There are the same old houses and things along the way, but by night, with the windows all lit up, it seems somehow more interesting and exotic.

As soon as we reach the edge of the field we can see Smokey, standing on the little hill in the distance. We call for him and he whinnies as he canters toward the fence. He's so happy to see us, he runs his head up and down my chest until he almost knocks me over. I put the rifle on the ground and give him a quick once-over, skimming my hands across his coat and down his legs to make sure he's fine. Cid scrubs his forelock and eases the bridle on. As always, Smokey takes the bit without a struggle.

"Go ahead and ride him first," I say, because I'm feeling generous now that we're with Smokey.

Cid grabs a handful of mane and throws her leg up and over with the ease of a rodeo rider. I have to smile thinking about that first time she rode him and could barely get on, hopping on one leg like it was a pogo stick. She gathers up the reins and urges him forward. Smokey is game, picking his way happily toward the gate. I grab the rifle and sling it over my shoulder, walking quickly alongside. I don't mind that I have to walk the first part of the way because it allows me to look at Smokey as he moves through the night. He's as magical as winged Pegasus with the moonlight dancing off his mane. Cid looks pretty good too, like some kind of pixie warrior-princess with her scrambled white hair and black-rimmed eyes. Smokey's hooves shine brightly as he walks, thanks to Queenie painting them with hoof black. She loves to do it and we all think it looks great, so she does it a lot.

By the time we reach the woods, Cid is ready to let me ride. I offer to carry the rifle over Smokey's withers but Cid takes it, allowing me to ride unencumbered. We don't talk, moving quietly through the starless black where the trees are so thick even the moon is hidden by the leaves. And though I'm thirteen now, I have to admit that these woods still give me the creeps. The night sounds and the darkness wear away my bravery until I'm thinking we should just turn around and forget about shooting the rifle altogether. But I say nothing and continue to ride until we finally reach the edge of the field, where the moon's face reappears and the darkness gives way to the low, enchanted glow of the meadow.

I dismount and tie Smokey to a tree branch, well away from where we're going to shoot. Cid unwraps the Winchester from the blanket and I pull the bullets from my pocket. It takes us a while to figure out how to load the rifle but at last we seem to have it.

"What should I aim at?" Cid asks.

I scan the field and see a dead cedar, shining like a bone against the dark trunks of the other trees. "Aim at that," I tell her.

Cid raises the Winchester to her eye, the way you see cowboys do in the movies. She takes careful aim and then she pulls the trigger. Nothing happens.

"I think you have to cock it with that lever," I say.

Cid pulls the lever down carefully until the rifle is fully cocked, then raises it to her eye again to sight the tree. She breathes in, holding her breath as she pulls the trigger. There is a terrible *bang* and the gun bucks and slams into Cid's shoulder, sending her flying backward through the air like a rag doll. I hear the air heave from her lungs as she hits the ground, and see her head snap back and then forward again as the rifle cartwheels end over end beside her. It falls into the grass and I pray that it doesn't fire that second round from the impact. But there is only a low *thud* as the rifle comes to rest.

I rush over to where Cid is sprawled out, the shocked face of the moon hanging over us in silent reproach. Cid lifts herself to her elbows, grass stuck in her hair and the black around her eyes smeared more than even she would like.

"Are you okay?" I ask, crouching down beside her.

Cid looks at me kind of dazed and rubs her shoulder. "Oh man . . ." is all she says.

For some reason this makes me laugh. And then Cid starts laughing too. Then we're both hysterical with laughter, rolling in the grass while Smokey looks on with his eyes all wide, wondering what the commotion is about. He probably thinks we're really hurt, we're making such a scene.

"You should have seen your face!" I say, my ribs aching and my eyes running with tears.

"I thought I got shot," she howls.

It takes us a long time to finally collect ourselves so that we can look for the rifle. The grass is so long I think we're never going to find it, but Cid eventually does and we inspect it to make sure it's okay.

"Who's 'Lazy Boy'?" Cid asks when she sees the writing scratched into the brass plate.

"I don't know. Maybe it was Dad's nickname."

"Dad wasn't lazy," Cid says. Then she gets all serious. "Are you still going to shoot it?"

Of course I am, and I tell her as much, but I'm ready for it. I aim at the tree, the same way Cid did, but I anticipate the jolt, resting the butt of the rifle against my shoulder so it can't slam into me the way it slammed into her. I hold my breath and squeeze the trigger. There is the terrible *bang* like before, and the gun kicks like a mule, forcing me back a step, though I manage to control it. I hit the tree too, right where I aimed. I turn to Cid, a big smile on my face, and she's smiling back at me. But then the smile leaves her lips and she gets all serious again.

"You can't bring Lazy Boy home."

I know it's true. I can't keep the rifle in my room because if Ma finds it, it's as good as gone. And then there's the chance that Queenie might find it some day while snooping around my things, and I don't even want to think about what that would mean.

"What should we do?"

"We can hide it," Cid says.

We spend the next half hour looking for a good spot to put the rifle. It's Cid who finally suggests the old cedar. There's a hole about five feet up. If I stand on my tiptoes I can just feed the rifle into the hole so that it nestles deep enough inside the tree to be hidden and safe from the rain.

When Lazy Boy is carefully stowed away, Cid turns to me. "Promise me you won't come out here shooting by yourself, Nat."

I open my mouth to protest but the look on her face is so sincere that I just have to concede. Even with all her eye makeup I can see that she's "in earnest," as Ma would say, and I have no choice but to agree. Again, I know she's right. I'm just not used to Cid making so much sense or being so concerned. It's odd, but at this moment I'm acutely aware that there is something unbreakable between us, something that holds us together, despite all the fighting and cruel words we've exchanged over the years. We're connected, Cid and me, in a way that's invisible and hard to explain.

We walk over to where Smokey is patiently waiting, his reins hanging loosely over the tree branch, the blanket that hid Lazy Boy in a heap on the ground at his feet. He could have bolted and run away with all the racket, but he chose to wait for us instead. He snorts and groans as I run my hand over his withers. I'm so proud of him, looking so beautiful and being so good, that I feel my heart begin to swell. I could stand here all night just admiring him. I take the reins from the tree branch and turn to hand them to Cid, but she's perched comfortably on a rock as though she intends to stay for a while.

"Do you want to try one?" she says.

I look at her kind of funny because I have no idea what she's asking me. She pulls a small packet from her coat pocket and I finally understand that she's offering me a White Owl Cigar. They're the little kind, with the white plastic filters and the ends dipped in sherry. Cid clamps one between her teeth and lights it. She puffs furiously until the tobacco glows orange. The smell is sweet and so familiar. I just have to try it. She smokes for a bit then hands it to me. I clamp it between my teeth the way Cid did and breathe in deeply. My lungs burn and I choke and cough until my face turns red.

Cid laughs and shows me how to do it correctly. I try it again and this time I get better results, although I don't know why anyone would want to do this all the time. The smoke smells nice in the air but it doesn't feel so good on the way in. I can't believe Dad smoked those big fat stogies. They must taste awful. I puff for a bit, just to make Cid feel as though I'm trying. I wonder if this is what she's been up to with that bunch of guys she's been hanging around with lately. It's curious to me too, why Cid would want to smoke cigars like Dad when all she ever says is that she hates him. I want to ask her, but I know she won't like being interrogated. Instead, I strike a pose like Clint Eastwood as The Man with No Name, and this makes Cid laugh. I look at her, smiling at me through the smoke, and even though I'm her brother, I can see that she has become beautiful over the last little while. I feel proud of her in a strange sort of way. I hand her back the cigar.

"I like it," I say.

"It's not so bad once you get used to it."

"Not the cigar, Cid . . . your hair."

Cid lowers her eyes and runs a hand through her hair. She pulls the plastic filter off the cigar the way Dad used to, puts it in her pocket, then tosses the butt to the ground, grinding it into the dirt with her shoe. "We should go," she says.

We take turns riding Smokey back to the field, but this time we talk the whole way. We talk about moving and what it will be like to live in an apartment. We talk about Lazy Boy and how it might have been for Dad growing up as a young boy in the prairies of Saskatchewan, and how he became a man with a family living in Illinois. We discuss all these things and more as we reluctantly leave Smokey in the field with the moonlight and walk home beneath the stars.

When we get there, it's as if we never left. Ma and Queenie are still snuggled together on the pullout couch. They have no idea we've been out shooting a Winchester in the meadow. Cid and I tread lightly past the living room and up the stairs. When we reach our bedrooms, I hesitate, thinking to ask Cid if she'd like to haul her sleeping bag into my room so we can camp out together and hold on to the moment we've found. But as I turn to speak, she's already slipping into her room and closing the door behind her.

Because it's so late, I climb into my sleeping bag with all my clothes on. There's no use getting undressed when I'm just going to have to get dressed again so soon. I lay my head down and look at the moon a little longer before I fall asleep in my room for the very last time.

chapter 4

creepy crawlers

I wake with a start to the sound of people thumping around in the hallway. The sun is blazing through my bedroom window. I jump out of my sleeping bag and reach for my pants before I remember that I'm still fully dressed. Opening my bedroom door, I see a couple of strange men moving boxes from Cid's room. The movers are here already. They nod at me and exchange curious smiles, which makes me close my door and check my face in the mirror. I'm a mess. I comb my hair quickly with my hands and go into the bathroom to brush my teeth. When I finally look half presentable, I go downstairs to see what everybody else is doing.

In the living room, Ma is giving the men instructions as to what to move next, even though the room is pretty much empty. I check the basement. It's empty too. The movers must have arrived ages ago. I can't believe I didn't hear them. All at once, I remember the bullets in the little cloth bag. Thumping up the stairs, I nearly crash into the men coming down with boxes from my room. I race through the door and frantically search around for the bag with Dad's uniform. I find it placed to one side and grab it with relief. But when I look inside, the cloth bag with the bullets is gone. This is not good. Did one of the movers take it? My heart starts to pound in my chest. How can I ask the movers if they took the bullets without Ma knowing? And if they did take them, they'll just deny it anyway, so I'm screwed.

I take the bag with Dad's uniform and go down to the kitchen. I find Cid and Queenie sitting on the floor, eating the only thing left in the house (Count Chocula) out of the only remaining dishes in the kitchen (two cracked bowls that I'm sure Queenie once used to mix her watercolours). Cid's face is washed clean of the black eye makeup, the safety pin is gone from her ear, and she has a toque pulled down to her eyebrows even though it's a hundred degrees out. With the toque on, you can't tell that she's done anything unusual to her hair.

"We get to ride in the moving van," Queenie says, like it's the most exciting thing to ever happen.

"That's nice," I say.

"And Ma said she's going to buy us a new saddle for sure! Do you want some cereal?" she asks, changing the subject. "There's still a little left." She holds up the box of Count Chocula and shakes it.

Ma must have bought it as part of her happiness campaign, because she wouldn't normally let Queenie sit down with a quart of milk and a whole box of sugary cereal without supervision. Even Cid is eating it and she hates marshmallows. She must be hungry.

"When did the moving men get here?" I ask.

"They've been here for hours," Cid says, talking into her bowl.

"Why didn't you wake me up?"

She looks at me as though I'm an idiot. "I was waiting to see if they would move you along with the rest of the junk."

"Ha ha," I say, trying to act nonchalant, but my mind is stuck on the bullets. I put the bag down and take the box of Count Chocula from Queenie. Instead of digging around for a bowl and spoon, I just pour the cereal into my mouth, then take a swig from the milk jug.

Cid shakes her head in disgust. "That is so gross."

"What's in the bag?" Queenie asks.

"Dad's old Marines uniform," Cid answers for me.

"Oh! Can I see it?"

"Ask him," Cid says, gesturing at me with her spoon.

I ignore Queenie's request and turn to Cid, talking through a mouthful of cereal. "Do you think the movers are honest?"

Cid raises her eyebrows innocently. "Why? Are you missing something?"

"Yeah, I am." I stop chewing to study her face and then the penny drops. "When did you take them?"

"Take what?" Queenie asks, looking back and forth from me to Cid like she's at a tennis match.

"Last night," Cid says.

"You came into my room?"

"Who took what?" Queenie persists.

"Where are they?" I demand.

"Somewhere safe, where no one will find them." Cid turns her attention back to her bowl of cereal.

"I wasn't going to use them."

"Use what?" Queenie asks. "What are you guys talking about?"

"Nothing," I say, tossing the box of cereal at Cid. She catches it with one hand and gives me a look.

"If you weren't going to use them, then it shouldn't matter that I took them."

She has me there. There's nothing I can do about it. At least the movers didn't find them. I should be thankful for that, I guess.

"What are you guys talking about?" Queenie asks again.

Just then, one of the movers walks into the kitchen. He's sweaty and kind of dirty from moving all the boxes but he looks friendly enough. He's wearing an orange cotton shirt with a patch that says "Allied." "Who's riding with us?" he asks.

Queenie jumps to her feet. "Come on, Cid!"

Cid scowls but gets up and follows Queenie all the same. "You coming for the big ride in the moving van?" she asks me.

I shake my head. "I'm going to walk."

"Suit yourself."

Cid and Queenie go with Ma and the movers in the van. I watch them get into the cab of the big, long truck. The man turns the engine over and the truck roars to life. It snorts and lurches, then pulls slowly away. This is really it, I tell myself as the truck groans up the street. I wander through the house for a bit, thinking of all the living that we've done here. I spend the longest time in my bedroom. The closet door gapes open, the wire hangers dangling from the rod. The movers have left scuff marks and footprints across the floor, along with little bits of paper and things. The room looks completely different now that all my stuff is gone.

When I'm done wandering around, I pick up the bag with Dad's uniform and leave through the front door. We'll have to come back to tidy the house before the new owners arrive, but for now, I'm more concerned about getting my room set up in our apartment. I haven't seen it yet, but Ma says that I'll have the sun porch to myself. I know the building. It's a big, red-brick Victorian four blocks up the hill toward town. I've passed it every day for the last five years on my way to school. It's nice enough and all, right across from the park. We're renting the apartment at the top. The family downstairs is a mother and two daughters, Ma says.

I walk slowly up the street. The trees are completely still, the sun pressing against the leaves and glaring off the sidewalk. I glance back at the house. The trumpet-flower vine is in full bloom, the brilliant orange bells nodding all the way up the stucco wall to my bedroom window. They seem to wave at me as I walk, as if they know that we are moving away.

When I can't see the house any more, I turn around and walk a little faster, toward the new place. Even if I didn't know the exact house, I would have no trouble finding it: the truck is parked outside and the movers are busy unloading things. I step aside to let them go up the stairs with our kitchen table then follow behind. The place is small, with a tiny kitchen, a bathroom, two small bedrooms, a cramped living room and the sun porch that Ma promised I can have as my bedroom. And that's it. Ma is busy cleaning and organizing the kitchen. In one corner of the living room, surrounded by a mountain of boxes, are Queenie and Cid. They're sitting on the floor watching the TV.

"Shouldn't you be helping Ma?"

Cid shakes her head, her eyes glued to the TV screen. "She told us not to do anything until the men are done bringing stuff in."

"What are you watching?"

"*True Grit.*"

It's a Western starring John Wayne—the actor Dad always called "The Duke." He's a one-eyed deputy marshal named Rooster Cogburn. He's squaring off across a big field with the bad guy, Lucky Ned Pepper, telling him he's going to kill him for the bad things he's done.

The Duke says, "I mean to kill you in one minute, Ned, or see you hanged in Fort Smith at Judge Parker's convenience. Which will it be?"

Ned says, "I call that bold talk for a one-eyed fat man."

"Fill your hands, you son of a bitch!" The Duke puts the reins in his teeth and kicks his horse, Beau, into a gallop. He's riding like a demon toward Lucky Ned Pepper, shooting and cocking the rifle with one hand, pistol firing away in the other. It's the coolest thing I've ever seen. Even cooler than when Han Solo outran the Imperial fighters in the *Millennium Falcon*. And the rifle he's shooting looks just like Dad's!

"Hey, look! It's Lazy Boy!" I say.

Then Beau gets shot and it's all over for The Duke,

it seems. He struggles to get out from under poor old Beau and I'm terrified, though I wonder if I could pull the same spinning and firing trick with the rifle. The Duke is saved by the arrogant Texan, played by Glen Campbell, who comes through in the end. Queenie cries when the girl's horse, Little Blackie, drops dead because The Duke rides him so hard to save the girl from a rattlesnake bite. I'm choked up too, but I know The Duke did what he had to do. The girl is saved and The Duke sees her safely home. As the credits roll over the image of The Duke, jumping his horse over the fence, Queenie turns to me, her eyes still wet with tears.

"Who is Lazy Boy?" she asks. "And what did Cid take of yours? She won't tell me anything."

I study her face for a minute. "You have to promise not to tell Ma."

Queenie crosses her heart the way she always does when she's swearing to secrecy.

"Lazy Boy is Dad's old rifle," I whisper. "I found it in that trunk in the basement. Cid took the bullets and hid them."

"It's for your own good," Cid says, like someone died and made her boss.

Queenie's jaw drops. "That's what you were doing down there . . ." She thinks about this for a minute. "Why is it called Lazy Boy?"

I explain to her about the name scratched on the barrel of the gun. But I don't tell her how Cid and I took the rifle out to the meadow to shoot it.

"Can I see it, Nat?" she asks.

I look at Cid and she looks at me.

"Yeah," I say at last. "But it will have to wait until we're settled in. I had to hide it."

Queenie gazes at me in awe, like I invented the rifle or something instead of just finding it in an old trunk in the basement. She crosses her heart again for good measure.

Then Cid pipes up. "Just to let you know, Queenie and I are taking the sun porch."

"No, you're not," a voice says.

It's Ma, standing behind us with her yellow rubber gloves, looking tired. I hope she didn't hear us talking about the rifle.

"Why not?" Cid demands. "It's bigger than the other bedroom. How are Queenie and I both supposed to fit in that tiny room?"

"You'll have to find a way," Ma says. "I don't want you girls in that sun porch, changing in front of the windows."

"But we can get curtains!"

Ma shakes her head. She's not going to budge on this one.

"It's so unfair!" Cid storms. "Nathaniel gets everything!" She jumps up in rage and tears the toque from her head, her white mop popping out like a clown gag in a circus show.

Now it's Ma's jaw that drops. "Your hair!"

Cid stomps out of the living room before Ma has a chance to comment. I pick up Dad's uniform and sneak off to the sun porch, leaving Queenie behind to contend with Ma.

I'm not in my room for more than two seconds when I hear a high-pitched scream. I tear down the hall to see what's happened and there's Cid, in the little bedroom, standing on top of a box and pointing in horror at the floor.

"Get it! Get it!!" she shrieks.

Queenie and Ma tumble into the room. I look at the spot on the floor where Cid is pointing. There's a huge centipede, frozen mid-flight by Cid's scream. It's so big, it looks like a cocktail weenie with legs.

"Eeeeeeeewwwwwwww!"

"Get it!" Cid screams again.

I charge the centipede and stomp on it with my sneakers. It bounces into the air like a flapjack and I stomp on it again and again until I'm sure it's good and dead. Then I lean over to inspect the damage. "Geeezzz . . . this thing has mass. I bet it weighs a pound or something."

"Get it out of here!" Cid says.

I'm not picking it up with my fingers, even if it is dead. I turn to get a paper towel from the kitchen but Ma has read my mind and brought one already. She doesn't say a thing, but snatches up the corpse with the paper towel and takes it to the bathroom to flush it.

"Probably clog the toilet," I say as I turn to leave.

"Ahhhh! There's another one!" Cid screeches, pointing to another spot on the floor.

I rush over and the thing bolts to get away but I chase it, stomping and shouting like mad. "We need another paper towel!" I call out to Ma.

The whole time I've been fighting the bugs, Queenie has been watching, her hand over her mouth in disgust. "Where are they coming from?" she asks.

Ma returns with the entire roll of paper towels this time and dispatches the second body.

"I am *not* staying in here with centipedes," Cid says.

Ma ignores her and I do a perfunctory inspection of the room, looking under boxes and along the baseboards and walls. "Can't see any more," I say.

I leave Cid and Queenie to their horror and go to my own room to do a quick bug check but find nothing. Looking around, I have to admit, the sun porch is nice. I can see why Cid wanted it. There's no closet, but it's surrounded with windows that look out over the park.

I can even see the cannons where I found Cheryl and Tyler kissing. Cheryl. How could I have been stupid enough to believe that a girl like her could actually like me? As it turned out, she just used me to get Tyler's attention. I feel a little ache in my heart, even though it's been six months since the incident happened. I try to tell myself that I really don't care, though I'm not sure I like the idea of the cannons right outside my window to remind me every night and day.

Pushing Cheryl from my mind, I consider the rest of the space. The floor and ceiling are made of wood and there is wooden wainscotting below the windows. It will be cold in the winter, no doubt, but at least we won't have to pay for heating, so we can get a little space heater and crank it. And we won't have to worry about the pipes freezing, either. I'm curious about the centipedes, though. How are they getting into the apartment? Maybe through the drains in the sinks. It could be worse, I tell myself. It could be rats. When we lived in Illinois, there were stories about little babies in the bad parts of Chicago getting bitten by rats in their cribs, or rats swimming through the sewers and coming right up the pipes into the toilets, biting people on the backside. That idea used to scare me. I've never heard of anything like that happening in Eastview, Ontario, thankfully. Besides, I don't even know if it's possible for rats to swim through pipes. Wouldn't they drown? Even still, I check the toilet every time before I sit down.

I'm musing on this when I look out the window and see some old coot staring back at me. He's standing in the top-floor window of the house next door and he doesn't seem the slightest bit embarrassed to find me staring right back at him. I can see now why Ma doesn't want Cid and Queenie sleeping here. If it's not one thing, it's another. I'll have to hang sheets or something in the windows before bed.

I place the bag with Dad's uniform in one corner of the sun porch just as the movers start bringing my boxes and the pieces of my bed into the room.

"Who's the old geezer?" one of them asks, pointing his thumb at the window.

"Better get some curtains, kid," another one says.

I nod and begin piecing my bed together. I try to forget about the old duffer in the window by thinking about the movie with John Wayne. I think about him cocking that rifle with one hand and shooting it, again and again. It's definitely the coolest thing I've ever seen and I'm determined to try it. The first chance I get, I'm going back to the meadow with Smokey to get Lazy Boy.

chapter 5
the new rig

We work hard over the next few weeks, organizing and unpacking and getting rid of more things to try to fit ourselves into our new life. The summer sun is getting hotter and hotter with each day, making the apartment seem even smaller, despite the fans Ma has stationed in every room. There are many more centipede sightings so I pretty much keep my bug-stomping sneakers on in the house at all times. Queenie finds a particularly big one on the back of a sponge while taking a bath one night and comes screaming out of the tub, totally naked and dripping water all over the kitchen floor. It gets to the point where I think I can feel them scuttling across my legs at night when I'm in bed, but I know I'm just imagining things. Ma thinks the people downstairs must be filthy and that the bugs are coming up through the heating ducts. I don't care why they're coming here, I just wish they'd stop.

Over the weeks it takes to settle in, Cid, Queenie and I sneak off to see Smokey whenever we can but it's not enough to satisfy any of us. Still, we know that we have no choice so we "grin and bear it," as Ma says.

Ma has been on a shopping spree lately. She seems to be getting a big thrill out of spending money, and she's spending a lot. I guess after years of scrimping and scraping it's natural to want to stretch a little. She bought Cid and Queenie whole new wardrobes. I got the Levi's and the Adidas sneakers that I wanted, along with a kangaroo jacket and some T-shirts, which I'm happy to have. I just wish Ma would be more careful with the money. We didn't make more than $10,000 on the sale of the house once all the bills were paid. I know because I saw the papers. It may sound like a lot of money, but the way Ma is spending, there won't be much left soon. It's all part of her happiness campaign, no doubt. But I can't help thinking of Charlie Chaplin's mother. I bet she spent all their money too.

Ever since I read that story about Mr. Chaplin and his "unstable" mother I've been keeping a closer eye on Ma. Especially since she's been acting kind of funny the last little while. It's not just the spending. She seems tired and stretched to the limit. She's even developed a strange cough. I know she's trying to maintain a positive disposition, but it all seems forced somehow. And she didn't even comment on Cid's hair, which is really odd. She's probably just trying to keep the peace, but

I'm concerned that she doesn't have the energy to kick up a fuss. She works as a secretary all day for old bachelor McKinley, a real estate lawyer downtown, then comes back at night to work some more, rearranging the furniture, waxing the floors, making curtains.

I don't know how Ma feels about Dad, but I don't want to risk upsetting her, so I decide to hide his photo in the drawer of my night table and his uniform under my bed so she won't see them by accident. I've put sheets up in my windows to thwart the old geezer next door until Ma finishes sewing the curtains. I've left one window uncovered—one that overlooks the park—because I like the view. I like the way the sunlight dances through the leaves and makes patterns over my walls. Cid and Queenie have been working hard too, getting their room together. I haven't heard too much bickering from their end of the house so it must be going okay.

* * *

By the time everything is organized and taken care of, a kind of sadness settles over us all. Things are comfortable enough. It just isn't going to be easy adjusting to life in a small apartment. Cid's been stealing away at night, to hang out with her friends and smoke, I bet. When we're not mucking around with Smokey, Queenie and

I languish on the couch, eating cereal and watching TV. I go downtown from time to time, just to hang out, but there's really nothing to do. Besides, I don't want to risk bumping into Cheryl or Tyler or any of their friends, and I sure don't want to see that old biddy Mrs. Geeter. She cornered me at the grocery store one morning when I was getting milk for Ma.

"Where's my paper, you lazy little devil!" she screeched, in front of a whole lineup of people.

"I don't deliver your paper any more," I tried to tell her, but she was determined to embarrass me. She pulled out her soapbox and went on about how I'd cheated her and such. I got fed up with her abuse and just left the milk in a basket in front of the checkout, leaving her to jabber away. Ma wanted to know where the milk was and I fibbed. I told her the store was out. I didn't want to explain how Mrs. Geeter had bawled me out because I knew Ma would take it upon herself to find the old bat and set her straight, which is the last thing I need.

Anyway, Queenie and I are lounging in front of the TV one Saturday morning when Ma springs a surprise on us.

"Let's go buy a saddle for Smokey."

Queenie flies off the couch to go wake Cid. I wolf down my cereal and pull on my sneakers. I know exactly where we're going. Thompson's Saddlery. Mr. Thompson makes the finest saddles in the whole country. His shop is on the edge of town and it's filled with the most beautiful things. I used to stop there sometimes on the way home from my paper route, just to look in the window and dream. I never had the guts to go inside because I know the tack is expensive.

Ma phones for a taxi to pick us up. I'm still tying my sneakers when Queenie shuffles dejectedly back from her room.

"Cid doesn't want to come."

"Why not?" Ma and I ask in unison.

Queenie shrugs. "She says she doesn't want to."

Ma goes to see what's up with Cid. Queenie sighs with disappointment.

"What's wrong with her?" I ask.

Queenie shakes her head. "She told me to leave her alone."

I can hear Ma's voice murmuring from Cid's room, then Cid yelling back. "Just leave me alone!"

Ma reappears, her lips clamped shut and her eyebrows touching in the middle. She's furious, but she's trying to control it. I can't believe Cid gets away with behaving the way she does. If it were me yelling and acting like a jerk, Ma wouldn't hesitate to deck me. She's always been easier on the girls.

"Let's go," Ma says.

"But why doesn't Cid want to come?" Queenie asks.

I intervene, grabbing Queenie's hand and escorting her down the stairs. Ma is not in the mood to field questions, and I don't want our trip to Thompson's to be cancelled because of Cid. I have a theory as to why she doesn't want to come. She's exhausted from staying up all night with her friends. She's too tired and ornery to think about a saddle or anything else right now. I'd like to smack her, she's so selfish sometimes.

We sit on the steps and wait for the cab. Ma says nothing so Queenie and I do the same. I can tell Queenie wants to talk about it but I give her a look and she gets the message.

The cab finally pulls up and Ma slides into the front seat while Queenie and I slide into the back. The driver speeds off, the cab weaving along the streets toward Thompson's. I'm enjoying the ride until I see a group of kids from school hanging out on the corner near the Bowlerama.

"What are you doing?" Queenie asks as I slump down in the seat to hide.

I don't want to be seen taking a cab. Only losers take taxis in Eastview. Everyone else has one, sometimes two cars of their own. At least the fare is only $3.50 this time. The driver drops the flag to stop the meter as we pull up to Thompson's shop. Ma pays and we climb out. I can't help feeling excited now. The bell rings brightly as we go in and there's old Thompson himself behind the counter, working on a saddle. I recognize him from the fairgrounds, but I didn't expect to see him here. I thought he'd have someone else working the shop. Everyone knows he has the nicest horses in the county. And he's rich. He's wearing his signature red plaid shirt and brown leather cowboy hat. His face is round as a McIntosh apple and his hands are big and raw as rump roasts. It's amazing to me that he can do such fine leather work with those paws.

"Morning, folks," he says, just like some old-timer from a western. With his cowboy hat and huge size, he kind of reminds me of The Duke.

"Morning," Ma says cheerfully.

Queenie's eyes are popping out of her head as she looks around the shop. There are show saddles of rich black leather, studded with silver. There are working saddles with big horns and matching saddlebags. There are saddles for everyday riding and trick riding and anything your heart could imagine or desire—all made by Thompson himself.

"What can I do you for?" he finally asks, finishing off some bit of work he was poring over.

"We'd like to purchase a saddle," Ma says.

Thompson sees Queenie drooling over one of the show saddles. It's black and shiny with all kinds of silver hardware. It looks like a million bucks.

"That one there is a beauty," he says, leaning against the counter and tipping his hat back. "Only made but four."

I lift the price tag and drop it like my hand's been scalded. The saddle is twelve hundred dollars!

"We were thinking about something a little less fancy," I say, to let Ma off the hook. I move over to the everyday saddles. "It's for a pony. Twelve hands high."

Thompson pulls a little saddle out from the back. It's made of brown leather that squeaks with newness as he carries it. It has plain wooden stirrups and a small, leather-covered horn, and although it isn't fancy, it looks quite serviceable. What's more, it's only a hundred and twenty-five dollars.

"Do you have one like that to fit a pony?" Ma asks, pointing to the show saddle Queenie was admiring earlier.

I open my mouth to say something because Ma obviously hasn't looked at the price tag for that particular "beauty." But she doesn't seem to notice me.

Mr. Thompson is more than happy to put the everyday saddle down and find something more expensive. He pulls out a little show saddle, just like the one on display only smaller, and places it on a stand for us to see. It really is a thing of beauty with its black leather-covered stirrups and embossed patterns decorated with silver. There are silver rosettes and fancy leather ties at the front and back for holding gear and securing saddlebags. And there's even a matching bridle that Mr. Thompson produces as if by magic. I touch the leather and it's cool and smooth beneath my fingers. I run my hands along the reins and I start to dream about Smokey sporting such a rig. He'd be the most beautiful pony in the world wearing this tack. I imagine myself riding him and everyone looking as if they were watching a show at the Calgary Stampede.

When I look up from my reverie, I see that Ma has already made the decision for us. She's standing at the counter, sharing some bit of humour with Mr. Thompson as he smiles and rings the sale through. He even takes the time to show Ma a couple of saddlebags that match the rest of the tack perfectly. I feel sick with guilt at the idea of Ma spending all that money on us. It's the nicest saddle I've ever seen, I can't deny that, but we would have fared just as well with something less extravagant. We've been riding bareback for nearly a year, so any saddle at all would be a luxury. Besides, we can't just spend all the money from the house and have nothing left in the bank. We'll end up worse off than we were before, now that we have no house to sell if things get tough again.

I look over to Queenie for support but she's too far gone for reason. She's staring at the tack as though she's seen an angel. This is like a dream come true for her and I should just stand down and let Ma buy the saddle. But thoughts of Charlie Chaplin's mother crowd my head and I just can't keep my mouth shut.

"We can't afford that saddle, Ma. The brown one is just as good."

To my horror, Ma brushes me off with a laugh. "Don't be ridiculous, Nathaniel." She turns to Mr. Thompson and continues to chatter.

Thompson winks at me and my face turns tomato red. He must think I'm an idiot. Despite my embarrassment, I still have no trouble noticing that Mr. Thompson seems completely taken by Ma, the way he's smiling and hanging on her every word. He throws in a nice little saddle blanket free of charge, and he even offers to deliver the tack to our house, but Ma won't hear of it. So he calls us a cab and carries the whole kit to the car, placing it carefully in Queenie's lap in the back of the taxi. He opens the cab door for Ma and closes it in a gentlemanly way once she's in. Then he turns to me and holds out his hand. He considers me thoughtfully as we shake, tilting his hat back the way he did before.

"You know, son . . . when I was your age . . . all I wanted was a hat and some cowboy boots. Now I've got the hat . . . and the boots . . . and a little bit more."

He smiles real big and I smile back. I can see that he's not a bad man. He didn't force Ma to buy the expensive saddle—she wanted to buy it. He had no way of knowing that we've been broke and scraping for years now. He himself was poor once—everyone knows that. I heard Dad say that old Thompson pulled himself up by his bootstraps, worked like a dog, and made millions. For a second I wonder if he and Ma could go out on a date. She seems to enjoy his attention. And she's been so lonely since Dad left. Maybe that's what happened to Charlie Chaplin's mother: she went crazy out of sheer loneliness. I've heard of that happening to people. I glance down at Mr. Thompson's hand and see a gold band around his ring finger. I feel myself blush again at thinking such a stupid thought. I thank him quickly and jump into the cab. He winks at me again as we drive away.

At home, Queenie insists on carrying the saddle up the stairs, even though Ma asks me to do it. She's practically tripping over the stirrups, she's so small. When we get inside the apartment, Cid is sitting at the kitchen table, leaning her head on her hands and nursing a glass of water. Ma totally ignores her, clattering around the kitchen to get lunch ready. She's giving Cid the deadly silent treatment. Personally, I'd rather get decked any day. But Cid doesn't even seem to care.

"Look what Ma bought us!" Queenie shouts before she even gets into the kitchen. "And we've got saddle-bags and a bridle to match!"

Cid looks up and squints at the saddle.

"Where'd you steal that from?" she says.

"We didn't steal it!" Queenie says. "Ma bought it from Thompson's! You should see his place. It has everything you could ever imagine. But we got the nicest saddle of all."

Cid actually makes an effort to appreciate the saddle.

"It's beautiful," she says. "It'll look nice on Smokey."

"We're going to try it on him today," Queenie says, like it's already arranged.

She just about has a fit when Ma says no. Ma thinks we should wait until we have a proper place for Smokey so that we can store the saddle and not have to drag it back and forth. Queenie begs like I've never seen her beg before and I count the seconds until Ma gives in. She only does because I promise to carry the saddle the whole way to Ted Henry's field and back.

I think Ma's relieved, actually, to have us out of the house so that she can gather her thoughts and relax a little. To my surprise, Cid wants to come too. We walk together, me hauling the saddle, Queenie with the bridle and brushes and Cid carrying the blanket and saddlebags. Queenie chatters away nonstop but Cid says hardly anything at all.

The saddle is feeling pretty heavy by the time we reach the field. I'm thankful to be able to put it down. I don't want to lay it in the grass so I place it carefully over a fence rail. I whistle for Smokey but he's already cantering down the hill to greet us. When he gets closer, I can see that his mane is a snarl of nasty old burrs.

Cid sighs. "It'll take us hours to get those out."

"We *have* to get them out," Queenie says. "We can't put our new saddle on Smokey with his mane all tangled. It'll look terrible."

I agree. We set to work, combing and brushing. With the three of us working away, it takes little more than an hour to get Smokey in shape.

"He looks good," I say, stepping back to admire him.

"Can we put the saddle on now?" Queenie asks.

"Yeah, sure," I say. "But we're going to have to go slow. I don't know if Smokey has ever worn a saddle before."

I bridle Smokey while Cid puts the blanket on his back. The bridle fits him perfectly and he looks amazing in it. Then I get the saddle, flipping the stirrups over the seat so they don't bounce around when I place it on Smokey's back. His ears lie flat as I lower the saddle over the blanket.

"Easy, boy."

"I don't think he likes it," Queenie says.

Smokey turns and looks at the saddle. He sniffs it warily as I reach under his belly for the cinch and slowly begin to tighten it. Smokey puffs up, just like any horse would, which makes me think he's worn a saddle before after all. Horses do it so the cinch can't be tightened all the way. I've seen handlers kick their horses in the belly to get them to exhale, but I would never do that to Smokey. I have the idea to lead him around until he forgets about the saddle, then tighten it afterwards. But as soon as I cluck for him to get along, he dances to one side, his eyes all wide, his ears still pinned against his head like he's never seen a saddle in his life.

"He's terrified," Queenie whines.

"He'll be all right," I say. I lead him around and around, until my arm is sore. When Smokey is walking calmly, I tell Cid to distract him while I work on the cinch. Smokey tries to nip at my hands.

"Hold his head," I say.

"I *am* holding his head."

"Hold it better, then. I have to tighten the saddle or it'll slip under his belly and send us flying."

Once I've managed to secure the saddle, I tug on it to make sure it's tight. Smokey dodges to one side.

Queenie frowns. "He hates it."

"No, he doesn't," I reassure her. "It's just going to take him a little while to get used to the idea of it." I lower the stirrups slowly.

"Can I get on him?" Queenie asks.

"Better let me go first."

"I want to go first," Cid says.

"Suit yourself." I hand her the reins. "Do you want me to lead him around for a bit?"

Cid doesn't answer but just takes the reins and puts her foot in the stirrup.

"Better make it fast," I warn. But before the words even leave my mouth, Smokey bolts. Queenie gasps as Cid holds on for dear life, one foot in the stirrup, hands clutching the saddle like she's some kind of trick rider. Smokey gallops across the field, mane and tail flying. Cid manages to lift her free leg over Smokey's back while reining him in. He tosses his head, champing at the bit, skipping and prancing left and right. Cid gives him a little kick and Smokey bursts into a gallop again. She rides straight toward us, then veers to the left and tears up the hill. Queenie gives a cheer as Cid canters Smokey along the fence and back to where we're standing.

"Geez, you should stay out all night more often," I say.

Cid doesn't answer. She kicks Smokey and off they go for another gallop.

"Give me a chance," I say, as they come around again.

I do the same as Cid, riding Smokey until I'm sure he's calm enough for Queenie. But when I go to help her on, she insists on doing it herself. To my amazement, she's up and on him before I can say Jack Robinson. She canters Smokey around, as confidently as Cid and I did.

"Oh, Nat," she finally says. "Isn't it all just so beautiful?"

I smile in agreement as I rub Smokey's neck. And then I get an idea.

"You know what would be cool?" I say. "It'd be cool to try to ride Smokey the way John Wayne rode Beau in *True Grit*."

"What do you mean?" Queenie asks.

"You know . . . shoot and ride at the same time."

Cid shakes her head.

"Come on," I say. "It'll be the coolest thing ever. We can do it in the meadow." I hand Cid the reins to persuade her. "You can ride Smokey on the way there," I say, to sweeten the pot.

"It's okay," Cid says, handing me back the reins. "We can take turns, just like always."

"Don't we need a rifle?" Queenie asks.

"We have a rifle," I say. "We have Lazy Boy. It's just like the one John Wayne used in the movie."

Queenie looks worried. "What if someone gets shot? What if Smokey gets hurt?"

"We're not going to do it for real, Queenie. We'll do it for pretend."

Cid scoffs. "And we may even have a few laughs when Nathaniel falls flat on his face."

"Ha ha, very funny," I say. "The Duke had to start somewhere."

chapter 6
the duke and a sour note

We let Queenie ride first so she can lap up the attention from the people who watch us go by on the street. You'd think it was a parade the way they gawk at Smokey. Queenie is having a ball, smiling and waving like she's Annie Oakley. We let her ride all the way to the meadow because Cid and I have no intention of letting her ride like The Duke once we get there.

As soon as we arrive, I check the dead cedar for Lazy Boy. It's there, tucked down inside the hollow just the way Cid and I left it. It seems fine, too. Dry, and not a scratch on it. I was a bit worried about squirrels but they seem to have left it alone.

Queenie whistles high and low, the same way Cid did when she saw the rifle. "That was Dad's?" she says.

"Ain't it a beaut?" I hold it up for her to see. She takes it gingerly, still sitting on Smokey's back.

"Is it loaded?" she asks.

"No! Geez, Queenie, do you think I'm nuts?"

"I do," Cid mutters.

"Give it here," I say, taking the rifle. I hold it the way

The Duke did in the movie and attempt to cock the gun, then spin it. The rifle slips from my hand and bounces to the ground. "It's gonna take some practice." I pick up the gun and try it again.

Queenie watches as I spin the gun over and over. She gets bored eventually and starts exploring the meadow on Smokey. Cid sits on a rock and oversees my progress, giving me pointers now and then. When I think I have it at last, I call for Queenie to bring Smokey over. She hands off the reins and hops down, sitting next to Cid on the rock.

"Go to the other side of the meadow," Cid says.

I get on Smokey and trot across the meadow to the other side, holding the rifle across my lap. When I reach the trees, I rein Smokey around and practise spinning the gun. Smokey shies when the rifle whirls through his field of vision but I hold him steady and continue to spin. He gets used to it a lot faster than he did the saddle. He's certainly more patient than Cid, who yells across the field for me to get on with it.

I practise a few more times then put the reins in my teeth, just like The Duke did. I breathe in and give Smokey a kick. He takes off and I cock and spin the gun. Queenie and Cid are cheering and shouting as Smokey and I get closer. I shoot and spin nine times and I've almost made ten when a stupid jackrabbit dashes out of its hole right between Smokey's feet. He bolts to one side and I go flying in the other direction, the reins nearly pulling my teeth from my head. I hit the ground like a ton of bricks. The last thing I see is the rifle arcing through the air and disappearing into the grass before the light explodes in my head.

When I come to, Cid and Queenie are leaning over me, looking all worried and asking if I'm okay. My head feels like a gong, the way it's clanging, and I can even see little stars swirling around like in the cartoons. "Did you catch Smokey?" I ask, my voice sounding strange to my ears.

"He's standing right next to you," Queenie says.

Smokey blinks back at me, looking as concerned as Cid and Queenie.

"It wasn't his fault," Cid says. "That rabbit flew out of nowhere."

I flop back into the grass and groan, rubbing my head. "Stupid rabbit."

"You were doing great, Nat . . . before that rabbit showed up," Queenie says.

"Yeah," Cid agrees, picking Lazy Boy out of the grass. "The Duke would have been proud." She hands me the gun.

"Don't you want to try it?" I ask.

"It's okay," Cid says. "There's been enough wild riding for one day, I think." She pats me on the shoulder.

I take a little time to recover, then stash Lazy Boy in the old tree. We take turns riding Smokey back to Ted Henry's field. When we get there, we remove the tack and give Smokey a good rubdown. He snorts happily, munching on grass while we brush him. As we pick up the tack and make to leave, Queenie turns to me thoughtfully.

"Do you think you'll try it again?" she asks.

I sling the saddle up onto my shoulder. "Oh, yeah," I say, even though my head is still throbbing.

"I promise not to tell Ma," she adds.

"That's good, 'cause she'd kill me." I squint against the pain in my head.

Queenie frowns. "Are you going to be okay?"

"Oh, yeah, I'm fine," I say. "It's Ma we should be worried about." Queenie's eyes darken and I regret my careless words immediately.

"Why should we worry about Ma?" she asks.

"Hey," I say, changing the subject. "Did you know someone stole Charlie Chaplin's coffin from his grave?"

My tactic works beautifully. Even Cid comes to life.

"What? How do you know?"

"I read it in the paper."

The girls listen intently as I tell the story about Mr. Chaplin's coffin being dug up and left in the woods. I tell them all about his life—except for the part about his mother—to stretch the story out as far as I can. Queenie is riveted, asking all kinds of questions that I can't possibly answer. Like, what did the body look like? And, did they bury Mr. Chaplin with his bowler hat and cane? I make things up, just to amuse her. We talk about it the whole way home, the story helping to shorten the journey and lighten our load.

"Do you think Mr. Chaplin's ghost is haunting the woods now?" Queenie asks as we tramp up the stairs to the apartment.

"I don't know. Maybe. Yeah, sure, I guess."

"Do you think his ghost will haunt the grave robbers until they die?"

"I wouldn't blame it if it did."

When we get to the top of the stairs, Ma is waiting for us.

"How did it go?" she asks.

Queenie throws her arms around Ma's waist. "He looked just like a picture, Ma!"

"Yeah," I say. "The saddle's great. Cid even did some trick riding."

"She was incredible, Ma!" Queenie says.

Ma smiles. "I'd love to see that sometime."

I guess she isn't angry any more. In fact, she seems to be in an extra-good mood, even though she looks pretty dragged out. She even has supper ready for us: lasagna, with real Parmesan cheese, which we all love, and a box of little powdered doughnuts from the grocery for dessert.

"Nat did a better trick than me," Cid pipes up. "He was riding like John Wayne."

I shoot her a look. But I can see by her face that she's just kidding and won't tell Ma what we've been up to.

"Sounds like fun," Ma says, then adds, "I have some good news."

Queenie claps before she even knows what it is. I put the saddle down and listen.

"I've found a place to board Smokey! A really nice place and it's not too far either."

"That's great!" we all say.

"Where is it?" I ask.

"Just up the road from Ted Henry's—one concession over, so you can still walk."

Ma tells us all about the new place and it sounds too good to be true. It's a *real* stable, with good stalls and working water and proper lighting, not like Ted Henry's junky old barn. I can't wait to move Smokey and kiss Ted Henry goodbye for good.

Ma hums happily, serving up big plates of steaming

lasagna. But as we tuck into our dinner, the strangest noise comes up through the floor and the linoleum begins to vibrate under our feet. It sounds like an old cow bellowing for her calf. We stop eating, forks poised.

"What is that?" Queenie asks.

"Sounds like the Phantom of the Opera," Cid says.

We listen some more. Cid's right. It's an electric organ. It must be one of the girls downstairs, practising. But she isn't very good. She keeps playing the same few notes over and over, ending with the same sour note each time.

"Sounds terrible," Queenie says.

"It's like that *Road Runner* episode where the Road Runner hits the wrong piano key again and again just to drive the Coyote nuts," I say.

"It's driving *me* nuts!" Cid says, throwing her fork clattering to her plate.

Ma's shoulders slump in defeat. She studies her dinner. "It's been going on all afternoon," she says.

We look at one another in shock. No wonder Ma looks so exhausted.

"Do you think she'll play every day?" Queenie asks.

"She'd better not," Cid says, scraping her chair from the table and tossing the last of her lasagna into the garbage.

I'm just about to launch into her about wasting food, but she retreats to her room, leaving the rest of us to rail against the bitter organ serenade.

"How come we never heard her play before?" I ask.

"She's been away at camp," Ma says.

The organ wails and staggers on. After an intolerable length of time, Queenie raises her eyebrows hopefully. "Maybe she'll get better with practice," she says.

This makes me and Ma laugh.

"I sure hope so," I say, knocking on the table for good luck, which makes us all laugh some more.

chapter 7
snobs

We get up early in the morning to go see the stable where we will keep Smokey. Ma has already spoken on the phone to the woman who runs the place so everything is pretty much arranged. She's going to meet us there to show us around and finalize the deal.

Ma calls a cab again and, curiously, it's the same driver that took us up to Thompson's the other day. I'm wondering if he's the only driver in Eastview, but nobody else seems to notice, especially Queenie, who's brought the sign we had made for Smokey at the fair last year, the old wire still dangling from the holes.

"Good thing it didn't get scorched when the barn burned down," she says.

It doesn't take too long to get to the stable. The fare is twice as much as when we went to Thompson's, though, and I'm thinking the driver has rigged the meter somehow. I watch as it clicks faster than the second hand on a clock, reaching eight dollars before we even arrive at our destination. But the moment we pull up to the lane, I forget about the fare altogether. It's obvious from a glance that this new place isn't at all like Ted Henry's operation. A big wrought-iron gate greets us at the entrance with a huge sign that announces Tanglewood Stables. Giant sugar maples line the laneway, throwing cool shade over the red-brick drive. The laneway alone is nicer than anything at Ted's. The taxi driver takes us in at a respectable speed toward the barn. Even he seems aware that this place is somehow different.

The stable is nicer than any house I've ever seen. It's made of fieldstone and brick, with arched doorways over every stall so that the horses can poke their heads out and watch life go by. In front of the building stands a beautiful bay horse in cross-ties, being groomed by a woman as expensive-looking as the horse. It's like something from Buckingham Palace. The woman is wearing green riding jodhpurs and black leather riding boots. She's braiding the horse's tail, and I think that she must be getting ready for a big event somewhere. I look at Queenie and she's gaping at the woman like she can't quite believe what she's seeing. Cid is slumped down in her seat, the way I was when we went to Thompson's. She's embarrassed to be pulling up in a taxi, and I don't blame her one bit, given that the other cars in the parking lot are mostly BMW and Mercedes-Benz. I'd be slumped down too if I could tear my eyes from the grandeur.

The cab stops a little too quickly next to a blue BMW, kicking up a cloud of dust. The woman looks disdainfully over as the dust cloud floats to where she's standing. She unhitches her horse and leads it through the open doors to the barn.

Ma pays the driver (ten dollars including the tip) and we exit the cab. I feel totally out of place already but I don't want to say anything to Ma. She worked hard to find a new home for Smokey, although I'm scared to think how much this is going to set us back. Queenie is gawking at everything and Cid is scowling, all ready to hate the place. This is not a good start.

We follow Ma into the barn and look around. The air is sweet with the scent of newly mown hay. You could eat off the floor, it's so clean. And the place is perfectly organized, with everyone's tack hung neatly on racks beside each stall, and the names of the horses engraved on wooden plaques above the doors. What's more, the horses themselves are stunning. These aren't just hackabout ponies. These are expensive show horses, prize winners and international champions.

I lean over to Cid, who's scowling even harder now that we're in the barn. "We're not in Kansas any more, Dorothy," I whisper.

Cid clenches her jaw muscles. I just hope she keeps

whatever she's thinking to herself, because Ma is happy about the situation and so is Queenie.

We stand in the aisle, feeling awkward, not knowing what to do next. We're like the Beverly Hillbillies, surrounded by all this opulence. Finally, a woman walks down the aisle toward us. It's the same woman who was grooming the horse outside. She seems way too young to own an outfit like this and I have to wonder how she came by it. I'll bet it wasn't by her bootstraps, like Mr. Thompson. This woman looks like she's never worked a day in her life.

Ma extends her hand and the woman takes it. She's wearing tan kidskin gloves.

"You must be Mrs. Estabrooks," she says in a British accent. "I'm Laura Mole. We spoke on the phone."

I stifle a snicker. How can she take herself seriously with a name like Mole? But it's obvious why. She's even prettier up close, with her pale, freckled skin and blonde hair. She reminds me of an expensive pastry from the French bakery downtown. Beautiful to look at but not too sweet.

"Have you brought the pony with you?" she asks.

Cid and I exchange a funny look because we know she saw us pull up in the cab. I'm convinced she said this just to irk us but decide to let it go for now.

"No," Ma says. "The children wanted to see the establishment first."

Now Queenie gives me a look. I don't think any of us are too sure of this. She begins to dip as though she's going to start into her funny little dance but I grab her by the hand and yank her arm, just enough to let her know that there will be no dancing anywhere near this place. She seems surprised, but says nothing.

"Well, let's have a look around, shall we?" the woman says. She gives us a formal smile and turns to walk down the aisle.

As we stroll past the stalls of champion show jumpers and walls of tack more expensive than anything we've ever owned, we are all but ignored by the other people in the barn, each as well dressed as the woman herself. She smoothes her hair with her gloved hand as she carefully explains the rules of the barn. There is to be no meddling with the other horses of any kind. Horses are turned out twice a day. The riding arena is free afternoons from one o'clock to three o'clock only. The rest of the day is reserved for classes. Hay is so much a month. Grooming and riding available for an additional fee.

When we reach a small stall near the back of the barn, the woman stops and addresses me directly. "Do you intend to join the Eastview Pony Club?" she asks me. "We're top overall in the county, twelve years running. Of course, your pony will have to qualify. We have our standards."

I squirm in my sneakers. "I'm not sure," I say, then blurt these next words out. "We don't need anyone to ride or groom our pony. We do that ourselves."

She smiles at me as though I've said something amusing, then gestures toward the stall.

"I think your pony, Molly, will be quite comfortable here."

"It's Smokey." Cid speaks at last, a tone in her voice.

Queenie proudly holds up Smokey's name plaque. "We have a sign for the stall already."

The wires dangle from the holes. The plaque looks ridiculous next to everything else in the barn and I wish that Queenie hadn't brought it.

"Yes, right," the woman says. "Well, I can't think of anything else at the moment. When did you say your pony will arrive?"

Ma speaks for us. "The children can bring him this afternoon."

I think she just wants to get the experience over with too. She pulls out her chequebook to pay, but the woman brushes it off, explaining that payment is due at the beginning of each quarter in three-month install-ments. Ma can mail in the first payment, as she herself doesn't handle the administrative duties in the barn. She smiles and extends her gloved hand again.

Ma shakes it and turns to go. We follow her out of the stable and walk past the fancy cars, down the maple-shaded lane to the big gate. Ma doesn't stop at the end of the lane. She continues to walk to the road, back toward town.

"Well, it seems like a nice enough place," she says at last.

Cid opens her mouth to say something sarcastic but I give her a sharp elbow before she can get a word out. I don't want her making Ma feel bad about the barn, even if the people are snooty. To be honest, Ted Henry's doesn't seem like such a hardship after all. At least we weren't made to feel like second-class citizens and "unfortunates" there.

"Aren't we going to call a cab?" Queenie asks.

Ma shakes her head. "It's a lovely day. We could all use a good walk."

I look at Cid and she looks at me. We both know to keep our thoughts to ourselves. I'm grateful, really, that Ma decided we should walk. I didn't want to hang around any more than Ma did, waiting among the expensive cars for a taxi to arrive while the people in that fancy barn made judgments on us. Still, we'd better get used to it, I guess, because we've agreed to keep Smokey there and we can hardly turn back now.

We walk along in silence the whole way home, lost in our thoughts. Queenie dances and skips along beside us but I don't do a thing to stop her. I'm too concerned about Ma. She seems so tired, so thoroughly broken. She starts to cough, from the dust and the heat, and can't seem to stop.

When we get home, Ma offers to make us lunch, but I say no. We can do it ourselves. Ma retires to her room with a headache. I hope she's okay. Cid, Queenie and I make peanut butter and jelly sandwiches, then grab our tack for the long walk back to the barn. At least we won't have to haul the saddle back and forth just to go for a ride. And who knows, maybe there are some nice people there.

"They can't all be snobs," I say as we make our way back up the hill.

Cid rolls her eyes. "Oh yes they can. Those people have never had to be nice to anyone. That woman didn't even take her gloves off when she shook Ma's hand."

"Maybe her hands are covered in a horrible festering rash," I say, just to be funny.

"What's a festering rash?" Queenie asks.

"If she has a festering rash on her hands it's from counting money her whole life," Cid says.

"She doesn't take care of the money," Queenie pipes up. "She said so in the barn."

"Yeah, sure," Cid scoffs. "That would be too vulgar for Miss Prissy Pants."

"She didn't seem that bad," I say, though my words lack conviction. "Besides, there's nothing we can do about it now."

"Don't you like the new barn?" Queenie asks.

"Yeah, sure we like it. It's just going to be a lot different from Ted Henry's is all." I heft the saddle to my shoulder to shift the weight.

"We won't be riding down the aisles the way we used to," Cid says.

"We don't need to," Queenie says. "We've got that huge arena to ride in now."

"Only between one and three o'clock," Cid reminds her in a prim voice. "A lot of good that will do us once we're back in school."

"It's going to be really nice," I reassure Queenie. "Look, there's Smokey, raring to get to his new home."

Queenie runs up to the fence where Smokey is waiting for us. Cid climbs over and I hand her the saddle.

"Look at his legs," she groans. "They're covered in

mud. And his mane is filled with burrs again." She tosses the saddle to the ground.

"Hey! Be careful!"

Cid ignores me and begins yanking the burrs from Smokey's mane.

"It's not his fault," Queenie says. "He can't help it if burrs stick to him."

"Well, we won't have to worry about this any more," I say, trying to be cheerful. "I'm sure there are no burrs at Tanglewood."

"Then why do they call it *Tangle*-wood?" Queenie asks.

"Ahhh . . . there's the mystery," I say. "It's a bit of high-class irony."

"Give me a break," Cid says, striking a snotty pose. "There's an additional fee if you want to board your pony tangle-free."

"Is that true?" Queenie asks.

I pull a clump of burrs from Smokey's mane and hold it up to Cid. "Hey, this kind of looks like your hair." I throw the clump and it sticks to her shirt. She throws it back at me and soon all three of us are throwing burrs.

"All right, all right! Truce!" I shout. "Smokey must think we're crazy."

He blinks at us complacently.

"I think he's rather amused by the whole thing," Cid says in her best impression of the Queen.

"He'll never be ready for the polo match if we don't hop to it," I say in my best Prince Charles.

"Will we have tea and crumpets afterwards?" Queenie joins in.

"Oh, yes, let's," Cid says.

We laugh and get to work, making sure Smokey looks presentable for his new home. We comb and fuss with his mane and tail for ages. The burrs are stubborn, leaving smaller and smaller barbs for us to contend with. Eventually we get them all out and Smokey looks magnificent once again. Queenie even polishes his hooves, and by the time we're finished, he looks like a million bucks. I saddle and bridle him, then hand the reins to Cid. To my surprise, she hands the reins to Queenie.

"You go first."

Queenie doesn't hesitate to jump on up. She's too young to know or care about what other people think. She rides as proudly as ever, all the way to the new barn, while Cid and I walk along beside her. I'm not sure what to expect from this new situation. I guess we will have to wait and see. I just hope that Cid doesn't cause problems with her attitude.

When we reach Tanglewood, Queenie dismounts and we walk Smokey into the barn. Right away there's trouble, because we have to walk past a group of girls in their riding breeches and blue velvet hats to get to our stall. It occurs to me that our Western show saddle from Thompson's is as out of place in this environment as a polar bear in the desert. The girls steal glances at us and snicker behind their hands. One girl speaks just loudly enough for us to hear.

"How *garish*," she says, emphasizing the word for full effect.

Thank heavens Queenie doesn't seem to hear or see any of this. Cid, on the other hand, is boring holes through the girls with her eyes and muttering something under her breath. I can't tell what she's saying but I know it isn't nice. I move her along with my elbow to prevent a scene. I don't want to start out on the wrong foot in this new place, especially since Ma made such an effort to find it and paid so much money for it too.

We remove the saddle and bridle and put Smokey in the stall. After we brush him down, I check the water trough and, of course, it works beautifully. Someone has even left some hay next to the stall for us. It's lovely—all green and baled to perfection. The sections fall away in neat leaves. It's sweet and has just the right mix of alfalfa and hay, so Smokey will no doubt approve, even though he's been grazing on grass these past few months. He tucks in greedily as I drop two leaves into his hayrack.

The tack I place on the wooden stand next to the stall. Looking at it there, I can see why those girls would snicker. It looks so loud with all its silver buckles and rosettes and such. I feel the colour start to rise in my cheeks as I think how proud I was only yesterday of this same saddle. I think about exchanging it, or saving my money and buying something more appropriate for this place. But I would never tell Ma. It would break her heart, especially since we were the ones who wanted a fancy saddle in the first place. I wonder what someone like Mr. Thompson would think of all this. He probably wouldn't care what a bunch of snooty girls thought. Then again, he's got so much money he doesn't have to answer to anyone. The Duke wouldn't care what a bunch of girls thought either. He'd just laugh and ride off into the sunset, leaving them to fuss among themselves.

Cid is leaning against the stall with her arms folded, staring at the floor. She looks up and our eyes meet for a second, and I can tell that she's hating every minute of this.

I'm about to say something when Queenie tugs on my sleeve. She's hung the plaque with Smokey's name from the metal bars on the door of his stall. It looks small and cheap hanging there but I don't tell her that. I just smile and say that it looks pretty good. She straightens it, then turns to me.

"Come on, Nat. Let's look around."

Cid follows reluctantly as we leave Smokey munching happily in his stall to inspect the facilities more closely. The paddocks are pristine. Somehow they're dry and still have grass growing in them, unlike others I've seen that are reduced to mud flats around this time of year. The fencing is neat and tidy, painted white from beginning to end and not a board out of place. The property must be huge because the fencing stretches as far as the eye can see. Next to the barn there is a big aluminum-clad riding arena. It's bigger than several houses put together. When we peek in, we see a couple of the girls from the stable, mounted and trotting regally along on their show horses. There are little jumps set up throughout the ring, and every once in a while one of the girls urges her horse over one or two. The whole thing is very civilized and controlled.

We watch the girls ride, Queenie all saucer-eyed and absorbed in the scene, until Cid loses her patience.

"Let's go," she says.

We check on Smokey before we leave and as I'm closing the stall door, I notice something scratched into our wooden sign that wasn't there before. Looking closer, I see the words "Howdy Doody" etched under Smokey's name.

"Why would someone write that?" Queenie asks.

This is too much for Cid. She storms out of the barn and over to the riding arena. She doesn't go in but waits until the girls are trotting past the door then bangs with her fist against the wall of the arena with a loud metallic crash. The horses rear into the air and several of them bolt frantically across the ring. I grab Cid and race back through the barn and out the front door, Queenie running in wild confusion next to us.

"Geez, Cid!" I say as we reach the road.

"They deserved it," she seethes. "Princesses."

"Why would they write 'Howdy Doody' on Smokey's sign?" Queenie asks.

"No reason," I say, trying to make light of it, but Cid has to open her mouth.

"Because they think we're trash with our Western saddle."

Queenie gasps. "But why?"

"Because it's not some prissy English saddle for riding around in an expensive arena. It's not high-class enough."

"But it cost Ma a fortune . . ."

"It doesn't matter," Cid snaps. "It's not the right kind of thing for those prisses . . . and neither are we."

Cid may as well have thrown a glass of ice water into Queenie's face. She retreats immediately into her dance, hunching over and moving her fingers in front of her face.

"It's not that bad," I say, trying to salvage the situation, but Cid is hard as stone.

"It's worse, Nathaniel," she says. "I'm not going back there again."

"What are you talking about?"

"I'm not!" Cid spits on the ground. "It's not worth it to be made fun of."

"But we can always get a different saddle."

Cid stops in her tracks, her eyes burning with rage. "Don't you get it? It's got nothing to do with the saddle. It's us . . . and Ma. We're not like those people and we never will be—no matter what kind of saddle we have. We're not their kind."

I think about this for a minute. Cid might be right, but the consequences are too hard to bear. If she lets those people get the best of her then she won't be able to see Smokey, because we can't ask Ma to find a new place.

"You can't let people make you feel that way, Cid," I say, sounding just like Ma. "There will always be people like that in the world. You just have to ignore them and get on with things."

But Cid doesn't want to listen. She spits on the ground again and folds her arms over her chest. For some reason this pushes me to say something I probably shouldn't.

"Maybe you just don't care about Smokey any more."

Cid looks at me with disgust. "What?"

"You're just using this as an excuse."

"You'd better shut up."

But I don't shut up. I keep going and make things worse. It's like a switch is suddenly thrown in my head and I'm not responsible for the words that come out of my mouth.

"You don't really care about Smokey. You'd rather hang around with your stupid friends, smoking and acting like a jerk!"

Cid grits her teeth like she's just received a big needle in the arm. But instead of saying anything, she lights out down the road, leaving me standing there in the dust with Queenie dipping and dancing beside me. I take Queenie's hand and continue walking. I don't feel angry any longer. I feel ashamed and cruel for what I've said. I just hope that Cid can forgive me.

chapter 8

ma gets sick

Cid is nowhere in sight when we get home. I can only guess that she is with her friends. I was hoping to apologize for what I said. Queenie and I even stopped at the variety store and bought Lik-m-aid candy for all three of us and some cans of ginger ale.

"Should we just leave Cid's on her bed?" Queenie asks, her tongue all purple from the Lik-m-aid.

"Sure." My own tongue is fire-engine red. Cherry Lik-m-aid is my favourite. I hand Queenie the goodie bag.

She carefully arranges Cid's can of pop and pack of grape Lik-m-aid in the bag, folding the top down neatly and putting it in the centre of Cid's bed. Then she takes a green crayon from her pencil case and writes CID in capital letters on the bag, decorating it with some flowers. When she's finished, she sits on the edge of the bed, dipping her finger thoughtfully into her package of Lik-m-aid.

"Do you really think Cid doesn't care about Smokey any more, Nat?"

I can tell she's been mulling this over the whole way home. It makes me feel like an even bigger goof than before.

"Oh, I was just talking stupid," I say, taking a sip of pop.

Queenie thinks about this for a minute. "Do you think Cid will ever go to the barn again?"

I sit down next to her. The truth is, I don't know. It's easy for me to ignore a bunch of snotty girls, but for Cid, it's different. It's hard to be laughed at. I can take it, even though it hurts me too. I just push it out of my mind and think of other things. But Cid can't do that. "I think she will," I finally say. "She just has to cool off a bit."

Queenie nods and jumps up from the bed. "I want to tell Ma about the riding arena."

"Don't tell her about the girls," I say. "We don't want her to worry."

Queenie nods and leaves the room. I make myself comfortable on Cid's bed, drinking my ginger ale and hoping that she will come home soon. Lying there, I have the opportunity to look at the girls' room carefully for the first time since we moved in. I'm actually impressed with how they managed to organize it, despite how small it is. They each have their own little area with a dresser and matching wooden shelves. Their clothes are hanging neatly in the closet, which they've divided invisibly down the middle, and their shoes are lined up with precision on either side. Queenie's little shelf is full of stuffed animals, with a few favourites displayed on the bed. Cid's shelf has some books and her makeup, plus her glass critters—or what's left of them since they got smashed when I hid them behind her dresser to get back at her last year. I'm happy to see the fawn that I gave Cid for Christmas in its little basket, placed carefully on top of her dresser. There are pictures and drawings hung on the walls and a poster of David Bowie on the back of the bedroom door. I'm marvelling at how they manage to keep the room so clean when Queenie comes shuffling back, a strange look on her face.

"Ma's not feeling well."

"What do you mean?"

Queenie just stares at me, so I get up and go to Ma's room.

Ma is there, hunkered down in her bed, the covers pulled up to her chin. Her eyes are shut and her face is sweaty.

"Ma . . ."

She doesn't answer. I put my can of pop down on her bedside table and place my hand on her forehead, the way she has done to me a million times over the years. Her face is warm.

"Ma . . . are you okay?"

She rouses. "Nathaniel . . . how did it go at the barn? Have you eaten?"

"It was fine, Ma. Just fine. Are you feeling okay?" I ask again.

Queenie stands in the doorway, wringing her hands.

"Can I get you anything, Ma? Some water? An aspirin?"

Ma shakes her head. "I'm just tired," she says, rolling over in the bed and pulling the covers over her shoulders. "There are leftovers in the fridge."

"We ate, Ma. It's okay."

I leave her there and go into the bathroom to get a washcloth for her face. Queenie follows me, practically stepping on my heels.

"What's wrong with her, Nat?" she asks.

"I guess she's got the flu or something. She's got a bit of a fever, I think." I turn on the cold water and run the washcloth under the faucet.

"Will she be okay?"

"She's just sick is all," I say. "She's been working really hard."

Back in the bedroom, I place the cloth on Ma's forehead. She gives me a little smile and clasps my hand in her own. She holds it for a while, until the smile fades from her lips and she drifts off.

"She just needs to rest," I tell Queenie as we tiptoe from the room. Closing the door, I remember my can of ginger ale on Ma's night table, but I'm not about to go back in and get it.

In the girls' room, I lie down on Cid's bed again while Queenie sits on the edge of hers. I produce Dad's old watch from my pants pocket and let Queenie inspect it while I fiddle with Cid's transistor radio, trying to find some good music. The local station is terrible. Most of the songs are old and sappy. They do have some good promotions, though, like the time they gave away a ten-speed bike to anyone found displaying their bumper sticker. I wanted to win that bike so badly but we didn't have a car to put a sticker on, so that was that. I thought about putting one on my skateboard then decided against it. Who would have seen it? Besides, it just would have advertised the fact that we don't have a car.

I tune the radio and Barbra Streisand comes in loud and clear, wailing over the wire, singing the love song from the movie *A Star is Born*.

"Turn it!" Queenie says.

I turn the dial, trying to find something better. Most of the stations are just static. I tune the radio back to Barbra Streisand because there's nothing else. "I wish I had one of those Sony Walkmans," I say. "They're really small and they have little headphones so you can listen to them anywhere."

"That would be cool," Queenie agrees.

Just as she says this, Cid appears in the doorway. "What are you doing on my bed?"

"Ma's sick!" Queenie says, before Cid can get mad at me.

"What do you mean?" Cid throws her purse on the bed. "Turn that crap off," she orders, gesturing at the radio. "Could you find anything worse than Barbra Streisand?"

"It was the only thing on." I turn the radio off and hand Cid the little bag with the Lik-m-aid and ginger ale.

She opens the bag and looks inside, raising her eyebrows in appreciation as she checks the flavour of the Lik-m-aid. "What's wrong with Ma?"

"She has a fever and she's been sleeping all day," Queenie says.

Cid looks at me for confirmation.

"I put a cold washcloth on her face."

Cid motions for me to shove over. "She's probably just worn out like the rest of us." She sits back and cracks open her can of pop, taking a few sips. "I'm sure she'll be fine."

But by the time dinner rolls around, Ma hasn't emerged from her room. I open the door to check on her. She's still sleeping. The washcloth has fallen to one side on her pillow. I go in and get the cloth, rinse it under the tap in the bathroom and place it back on Ma's forehead. She doesn't even seem to notice that I'm there. I shut the door and file a report to Cid and Queenie, who are in the kitchen, scrounging up dinner.

"Kraft or Campbell's?" Cid asks, holding up a box of macaroni and cheese in one hand and a tin of tomato soup in the other.

"KD!" Queenie shouts, as though Kraft Dinner is the best food in the world and we never get to eat it.

"Think Ma will want some too?" I ask.

Cid shakes her head. "Shouldn't feed a fever. She needs to drink lots of liquid."

I nod as though everyone knows this bit of expert advice. "I'll bring her some ice water."

I set to work getting Ma some water while Cid and Queenie make the macaroni and cheese. But Ma's sleeping so soundly, I haven't got the heart to wake her up.

"Did she drink the water?" Cid asks when I return to the kitchen.

"I didn't want to wake her."

Cid shakes her head as though I'm a simpleton and goes off to Ma's room. Queenie stirs the noodles and I get the margarine and milk ready.

The macaroni is served by the time Cid comes back.

"She didn't want to drink the water at first but I made her," she says, filling the glass again. "You have to drink when you have a fever or you'll get dehydrated."

"Okay, Florence Nightingale," I say, to make Queenie laugh. But Queenie just frowns.

"Will Ma be okay?" she asks as we sit at the table to eat. "Maybe she should go to the doctor."

"It's just a fever," Cid says. "It's not like Ma hasn't been sick before."

I nod in agreement and we dig into our dinner. It's only macaroni and cheese from a box but it tastes pretty good. I add ketchup to mine. Queenie and Cid think that's disgusting but I like the sweetness. As we're eating, the strains of the organ rise up through the floor.

"Oh no," I say. "That's the last thing Ma needs."

Cid sneers. "Aren't there laws against this? Isn't crappy organ music considered a form of noise pollution?" She pounds her foot on the floor in protest.

The organ music continues. It's the same crummy bit of song with all the same sour notes as before.

Queenie raises her fork in the air. "This is definitely worse than Barbra Streisand," she says.

★ ★ ★

The organ music groans on until eight o'clock. When it finally squawks to a stop, we look at one another with relief.

"Thank God," Cid says, her tongue purple from the grape Lik-m-aid. She throws her cards to the table.

We've been playing for the last hour to keep ourselves from going nuts with the music. Crazy eights's, appropriately enough. Ma somehow manages to sleep through the racket, though I can hear her coughing from time to time. I check on her often, changing the cloth on her head. She barely moves during my feeble ministrations. Her face seems to be getting hotter as the night wears on, and her cough is sounding worse.

"She should drink more water," Cid says. She gets up from the table and runs the tap as she cracks ice cubes from the tray and drops them into a tumbler. She fills the glass and carries it to Ma's room.

When Cid is gone, Queenie turns to me with a face as sober as Sunday morning. "Is Ma going to be all right?"

"Geez, Queenie. It's just a fever!" I say. But to be honest, I'm starting to get scared. Is this the way it went with Charlie Chaplin's mother? Spending money and pretending to be happy, working too hard and eventually becoming sick until she was unstable and institutionalized and the children were left to fend for themselves?

Cid returns with an empty glass. "She drank the whole thing," she says, refilling the tumbler under the tap.

Queenie and I look up hopefully.

"Did you ask if she wants anything to eat?" I ask.

Cid shakes her head. "Maybe in the morning."

We play cards for a while longer then watch a rerun of *The Carol Burnett Show*. It's the one where Tim Conway is a galley slave on a Viking ship.

"Ma *loves* this one," I say, laughing as Tim Conway tries to pick up a piece of bread with his filthy feet.

"She'll be sorry she missed it," Queenie says.

After the show, I turn off the TV and we all just sit there.

"Want to play Yahtzee?" Queenie asks.

"Nah, I'm going to go to bed," Cid says.

I thought for sure she would want to sneak off and hang out with her friends. She must be more worried about Ma than she's letting on.

"I'm going to bed too," I say. I get up and go to the bathroom to brush my teeth.

By the time I'm finished, Cid and Queenie are already settled in their room. I can hear them talking as I lie in my bed, watching the leaves dance in the light from the street lamp. I imagine Smokey in his stall at the new barn. I wonder if he is confused by his new surroundings. I hope he isn't scared. We didn't even say goodbye to him when we left. He must wonder what's going on. Then I think about Ma, lying in her bed. After a while I get up to go check on her and find Cid already there. She puts her finger up to her lips.

"I think she's feeling better."

"How do you know?"

Cid shrugs and closes the door. "She seems to be sleeping soundly."

"What's going to happen tomorrow?" I ask.

"What do you mean?"

"Ma has to go to work." I realize how stupid this sounds after it comes out of my mouth.

"We'll call her boss and tell him she's sick," Cid says.

"Yeah, of course," I say, like it's the obvious thing to do. I creep back to my room and lie down on my bed again. I watch the leaves for a while longer before falling asleep.

chapter 9
i'm a jerk—again

In the morning, I find Cid in the hallway peering into Ma's room. "Did you even go to bed?" I ask.

Cid ignores me.

"Is Ma any better?"

Cid closes the door quietly. "She's still sleeping."

"Still? Did you talk to her?"

"I made sure she drank something."

"I think she needs more than just water, Cid . . . at least some aspirins or something."

"I gave her some aspirins."

"Well . . . maybe she needs something stronger. She can't just lie there all day."

"Lower your voice," she says, just as Queenie appears, rubbing the sleep from her eyes.

"How's Ma?"

"Better," Cid says.

"Can I go in and talk to her?"

"Not right now. She just got back to sleep."

"I had a bad dream about Frankenstein," Queenie says. "He was chasing us through the woods and I was trying to run but I couldn't because the ground was too soft and all I had on was my underwear and bare feet. And then we were back in the yellow house but we couldn't find Nat and I thought the monster got him . . ." She shivers and rubs her eyes some more.

"It was just a dream," I tell her.

"What time are we going to see Smokey?" she asks.

I turn to Cid for an answer.

"I'm not going to go," she announces.

"What? Why not?"

"Someone should stay here with Ma."

Queenie's jaw drops. "I thought you said she was feeling better." She reaches for the handle on the door to Ma's room.

I put my hand on her shoulder to stop her. "Come on . . . it's okay. We'll have fun. Maybe we can ride Smokey in the arena."

"You can use my skateboard," Cid offers.

This seems to work. Queenie's been wanting to learn how to ride a skateboard ever since I got mine. She goes off to her room to get dressed.

"We have to call Mr. McKinley and let him know that Ma won't be in," Cid says.

What she really means is that *I* have to call Mr. McKinley. Cid hates talking to people.

I pick up the phone and dial. I don't have to look the

number up, because I've called Ma at work enough to have it memorized. I've never called this early before, though, so I have no idea what to expect. The phone only rings once before it's answered by old McKinley himself.

"Hello?"

"Mr. McKinley . . . it's Nathaniel Estabrooks. I'm calling to tell you that my ma is sick and she won't be in today."

"I'm sorry to hear that," he says, like I'd just told him that his favourite brand of canned soup had been discontinued. I can just see him in his dingy office with the peeling wallpaper and Dictaphone from the Dark Ages. He's so cheap, he hasn't bought a new piece of office equipment since Edison invented the light bulb. He clears his throat but says nothing. You'd think words cost money by the way he's rationing them out. Maybe I haven't explained things clearly enough.

"I don't know when she'll be in," I continue.

"Oh. I hope it's nothing serious," he says.

"We're not sure."

McKinley asks a few standard questions about Ma's condition. I give him as much information as I can. He's polite and all, but I suspect he's feeling as inconvenienced as Ebenezer Scrooge to have his clerk off during business hours. He expresses his concern and tells me to give his "regards" to Ma. I almost burst out laughing when he says this. You'd never know Ma's been working for him for the last four and a half years.

"What'd he say?" Cid asks.

"Nothing. He's such a weirdo."

"Well, you'd better get going. Smokey will wonder where we are."

The trip to Tanglewood takes a long time, not just because it's farther away, but because I'm teaching Queenie how to skateboard. She's fallen off about fifty times already, but I have to give her credit, she just keeps getting back up and on the board again.

"I want to be like that guy who rides empty swimming pools," she says as she rolls at a crawl along the street.

"Who? Tony Alva?"

"Yeah," Queenie says.

I skate past her, jump the curb and kick my board. "First you have to learn how to go in a straight line without falling off."

Just as I say this, Queenie hits a pebble and goes shooting forward, the board rocketing out behind her, causing a car to swerve dangerously. The driver shouts something out the window that sounds like "Watchit, ya stupid kids!" Queenie looks despondently up at me from the street. "I think maybe we should walk for a while."

I help her up, rescue Cid's board and hold it by the wheels along with my own. A Dickie Dee ice cream cart jingles past. Queenie looks at me hopefully but I haven't a penny in my pockets. "We'll get one next time," I promise.

We say nothing the rest of the way to the stable, both of us absorbed with desire for ice cream.

"Do you think Cid really stayed home because of Ma?" Queenie asks as we finally reach the big gates.

"Of course. Why else would she stay home?" I say this matter-of-factly. But I know what she's really thinking because I'm thinking the same thing. She's worried that Cid will never come to the barn again on account of those girls. Walking down the lane, we see the same expensive cars parked out front and I feel myself start to panic. Maybe Cid is right. Maybe we just don't fit in.

When we reach the door, Queenie steps into the barn as though she belongs there. She clumps along the length of stalls, admiring the other horses. I skulk alongside her, hoping the girls are already out riding in the arena. To my dismay, they aren't. They're gathered in a group at the end of the aisle. Queenie smiles and waves cheerfully. The girls seem taken aback by this and a couple smile and wave—out of politeness, I guess. I wave half-heartedly and make a beeline for Smokey's stall.

He nickers excitedly when he sees us and suddenly I don't care about the snotty girls. I open the stall door and he walks toward me, pushing against my pockets with his muzzle. He knows I have an apple for him. I hold it out in my hand and he happily munches it down, his eyes half closed with pleasure. When he's done eating the apple, I get his halter and put it on him.

"Can you put him in cross-ties?" I ask Queenie. "You can pick his hooves and brush him while I clean the stall."

Queenie leads Smokey to the cross-ties. He looks excitedly from stall to stall, eager to meet the other horses. I go down the aisle to the end of the barn and grab a neat little wheelbarrow and a pitchfork. The wheelbarrow looks as though it's hardly been used, and it's so small, it doesn't seem practical. I guess high-class horses don't make much of a mess. I shrug, place the pitchfork in the barrow, and trundle it along the aisle, stopping to look out a sparkling clean window at some riders doing figure eights in a small corral outside the barn. They have perfect form and move with great confidence. It looks like a scene from *National Velvet*. My heart sinks at the sight of it because I really don't want these girls to see me ride. I come from the John Wayne school of horsemanship and I'm sure they won't approve of my cowboy style. I already know what they think of our saddle.

When I finally pull myself away from the window, I see Queenie talking to one of the snobs. The girl is smiling and laughing. What could they possibly be talking about? The girl takes off her riding helmet and puts it on Queenie's head, showing her how to adjust the straps. Queenie is beaming like it's Christmas. For some reason this makes me furious. Is she making fun of my sister? I rattle the wheelbarrow angrily down the aisle, the pitchfork bouncing and clanging inside.

"What's going on?" I demand as I jerk the barrow to a stop in front of Smokey.

Queenie spins around, a huge grin on her face. "Alyson is showing me how to wear a riding helmet! She's going to teach me how to ride English and she even has a little saddle that will fit Smokey perfectly!"

I turn to look at Alyson, my mouth gaping like I'm the village idiot. She looks back at me, as cool and collected as a queen. She's maybe sixteen or seventeen but she has the confidence of someone much older and decidedly privileged. I search her face for deception, her grey eyes reflecting the light, her gold hair pulled back in a perfect little knot at the base of her neck. Her skin is smooth as porcelain and her lips are like two pink flower petals. She stares at me unflinching, and my anger blurs into shame. I can't think of a single thing to say and I'd rather wrestle the hounds of hell than face the scrutiny of this beautiful girl. What's more, I can't stop myself from being attracted to her. Suddenly

I wish that I were anywhere else but here. Am I to be tortured by girls like Cheryl my whole life?

"It's okay, isn't it, Nat?" Queenie says, bursting into my anguished thoughts. "Alyson's going to show me the *proper* way to ride."

The word "proper" stirs up my anger again, at least enough for me to reclaim my pride. "How's that?" I say in response to Queenie but still looking at Alyson.

Alyson folds her arms and tilts her head slightly to one side. "English," she says.

She has a British accent, like the woman who runs the place. Is everyone related around here?

"Your sister may have a precocious talent and it's best to start young."

"Precocious talent?" I repeat the words in my best John Wayne imitation.

"Yes," Alyson continues. "If she's to achieve any level of expertise, it would be wise to begin as early as possible. Besides, this type of instruction is beneficial both mentally and physically."

Mentally and physically? "What are you driving at?" I say, thinking she's referring to Queenie's dancing.

"I beg your pardon?"

I lower my voice so Queenie won't hear me. "You think she's deficient."

"I never said anything of the kind. I'm only trying to help."

"And how much do you charge for that?"

Alyson's face registers a mixture of confusion and indignation. "Charge? I meant it as a favour."

"Oh . . ." Once again I feel like a big creep. What a jerk she must think I am! I stammer away, trying to right the situation. "Well . . . sure . . . I mean . . . if Queenie is interested . . ."

Queenie jumps up and down, clapping her hands excitedly. "Yes, yes, yes!"

Alyson gives me a pointed look. It's just a glance, laced with the smallest amount of judgment, but she may as well have jabbed me with a knife. How could I have been so stupid? She was just being nice and I assumed that because she's pretty and rich she must be up to something. Maybe Queenie could benefit from some instruction. Maybe it would even help her to stop dancing . . .

I leave Queenie and Alyson in the aisle and trundle the wheelbarrow to Smokey's stall. As I'm working away, it seems somehow fitting that I should be mucking steaming manure after the way I just acted. I'm so used to defending Queenie that I'm always on the attack. I can't even tell when people are just being nice. I hate myself sometimes! Despite my humiliation, I can't stop myself from glancing up once in a while to watch Alyson with Queenie. She helps her saddle Smokey and adjust the stirrups, then shows her the correct way to mount and dismount. Queenie is clearly ecstatic, hanging on Alyson's every word and pouring her heart and soul into the lesson. What's worse, Alyson seems genuinely nice and patient and caring, like an older sister or something. My face burns with guilt as I pitch a particularly large forkful of manure into the barrow.

The pile in the wheelbarrow leans dangerously to one side. In my efforts to avoid the girls, I've emptied the entire stall of straw, dirty and clean. Now the little wheelbarrow is full to the tipping point. I wait until Queenie and Alyson unhitch Smokey and lead him into the arena before commandeering the wheelbarrow from the stall. I struggle to navigate the aisle to the manure pile. I'm just about out the door when I stumble and the whole load capsizes. I look up in horror to see the National Velvet riders watching me.

"That wheelbarrow is meant for hay," one of them says with contempt.

My face burns as I right the barrow and begin shovelling the mess one forkful at a time onto the manure pile. When I'm done, I quickly brush out the wheelbarrow with my hands then return it and the pitchfork to their respective spots. I fill Smokey's trough with hay, pulling the stray strands from his water bowl. I check his salt lick (included in the cost of the rent) and fluff clean yellow straw around the stall. When I've done everything I possibly can to keep myself busy and there's nothing left for me to mess around with, I decide to swallow my pride and see how Queenie is doing in the arena. Too embarrassed to actually go in, I loiter in the doorway and watch as Alyson puts Queenie and Smokey through their paces.

I'm amazed to see that Queenie is a natural, riding around the ring, heels down, posting like she's done it her whole life. Smokey trots like a thoroughbred in the English saddle. It seems to fit him perfectly and I have to admit that it does look sophisticated. Alyson is standing in the middle of the ring, calling out instructions. When she sees me watching from the doorway, she indicates that Queenie should stop and walks over to where I'm standing. Queenie rides alongside her, a huge grin on her face.

"He did really well, didn't he?" she gushes.

Alyson smiles, then turns to address me. "She's going to need proper footwear," she says, as though I'm Queenie's father or something. "She can't ride in sneakers. It's not safe. She can borrow the saddle and helmet until she gets her own. Smokey will need the correct bridle as well."

"Do you want to take a spin around the ring?" Queenie asks me.

I shake my head. I've embarrassed myself enough for one day.

"Alyson says that I can learn to jump, too, once I have my seat. And she says we can go on hacks together if I want to."

"Hey, that's great," I mutter, trying to sound enthusiastic.

They lead Smokey into the barn to brush him down, laughing at something together, while I wait, leaning against the wall. When they are finished grooming Smokey, Alyson unclips the cross-ties and Queenie leads him into his newly cleaned stall. She hesitates before removing his halter.

"You're sure you don't want to ride today?" she asks.

"Yeah, I'm sure," I say. "Besides, we should get home to see how Cid's doing with Ma."

Alyson walks up to us, the saddle over her arm. "I can give you another lesson next time you're here, if you like," she says. She smiles fondly at Queenie then gives me a disinterested look and says, "See you." Just like that.

The walk home is arduous. It's sweltering and the cicadas are sawing in the trees. Queenie is too hopped up to ride the skateboard. In fact, she could care less about the skateboard now. This morning she wanted to be the next Tony Alva and this afternoon she's forgotten he even exists. She's jumping and skipping beside me, talking a thousand miles an hour. Alyson this and Alyson that. I feel like I'm going to scream if I hear that name one more time. Instead, I just tune Queenie out, hmming in response every once in a while to be polite.

"I *know* it wasn't *Alyson* who wrote 'Howdy Doody' on Smokey's sign," Queenie says. "She's *way* too nice to do something like that."

"A-huh . . ."

"And isn't she just beautiful? She's from *England*. I want to wear my hair just like her, in a little bun at the back. Her eyes are grey—did you notice?"

"A-huh . . ."

"She's so nice. Even Cid would like her. Maybe they can be friends, and Alyson can teach Cid how to ride *properly.*"

"Queenie!" I finally snap. "Enough! I can't take it any more."

She looks at me like I've got two heads. "What's wrong with you?"

"Nothing! Absolutely nothing." I run my hands through my hair. I don't even know how to express the way I'm feeling. My heart is churning with a mixture of frustration and jealousy and confusion. "Alyson is great—honestly. She really is. I'm glad you had a good time today. I'm just not in the mood to listen to you talk about her for the rest of the day is all."

Queenie furrows her brow. She folds her arms across her chest and walks on in silence. I feel like a creep but I can't help it. I've had enough for one day. Besides, we can't burst into the house all excited and happy, talking about this and that and how much fun we had, after Cid spent the whole day inside, taking care of Ma. Queenie starts to dip and dance beside me. I don't even care.

We're walking like this when I think I see Cheryl and Tyler zipping past in his parents' yellow convertible. I grab Queenie and haul her behind a tree until they pass. Queenie pulls away from me and marches the rest of the way home without saying a word.

chapter 10
tragedy

Queenie and I return home to find Cid sitting on the edge of Ma's bed.

"How's Ma?" Queenie asks, peeking into the room.

Cid waves us quiet as she gets up to meet us in the hallway, closing the door softly behind her. She motions for us to follow her to the kitchen. We gather around the table.

"She's not feeling any better," Cid says.

"Did you talk to her?" I ask.

"Just a little. She won't eat anything. She just keeps saying that she feels tired."

"But she's been sleeping and sleeping!" Queenie blurts out.

"Maybe we should call the doctor," I suggest. "Do we have his number?"

"Should be in the phone book," Cid says.

I move into the living room and find the phone book. It's the same old one with the cover missing. I tore it off last year after using it to write on when we went to get Smokey. I wonder why we haven't gotten a new phone book as I flip through to the physicians section. Our family doctor is the first in the list: Abrahams. I dial the number and wait for the receptionist to pick up. The phone rings and rings. Then it dawns on me why no one is answering.

"It's after hours," I tell Cid. "They won't be back until tomorrow morning." I hang up the phone. "Are you sure Ma isn't feeling any better?"

Cid sighs with frustration. "I told you she isn't. If you don't believe me, go check for yourself."

It's not that I don't believe Cid. I guess I'm just hoping that everything is really okay and that we won't have to call anybody. I open Ma's door quietly, and when I see her up close, I know Cid is right. Ma doesn't look good at all. I sit on the edge of bed the way Cid was doing when we came home. The washcloth I had soaked and placed on Ma's head earlier is crumpled to one side of her pillow. There is a glass of water on the bedside table, untouched.

"Ma?"

She doesn't move.

"Ma?"

When she still doesn't answer, I reach over and shake her arm, the panic rising in my heart. "Wake up, Ma."

Ma's eyes flutter and her head lolls over on the pillow. She's shivering and covered in perspiration. "Nathaniel . . ."

"Ma, you have to get up. You have to eat."

"Are you hungry? I don't feel well," she murmurs.

"No, Ma, I'm fine. You have to get up and take a bath or something." I feel so stupid saying this but it's the only thing I can think of.

The situation is too much for Queenie. She starts to blubber. Cid hustles her off to the living room but I can still hear her crying.

"I'm going to call someone, Ma . . . a doctor or someone to come and see you."

"I have to get up for work," Ma murmurs.

"It's okay, Ma. I phoned Mr. McKinley. He knows that you're sick and won't be in."

Ma begins to cough. I take the washcloth and freshen it with cold water from the bathroom sink. I wring it out and bring it back to Ma's room, placing it gently on her forehead. I close the door carefully as I leave and go into the living room, where Cid has managed to get Queenie to stop crying. She's still sniffling, though. Cid and I exchange glances as I open the phone book again.

"Who are you going to call?"

"The hospital. Maybe they can send someone over."

Queenie bursts into tears again, covering her face with her hands. "They're going to come and take us away," she wails.

"What? Who?"

"The Children's Aid!"

Cid looks at her in shock. "The Children's Aid is not going to take anybody away."

"Yes, they will," Queenie insists between sobs. "That's what happened to Jimmy Perusitto and his brother when his parents got killed in a car crash. The Children's Aid came and took them away and now they'll never see each other again." She cries harder than ever.

"Who told you that?" I say, dialling the number to the hospital. The switchboard answers and immediately puts me on hold. Canned music filters through the earpiece—some Muzak version of The Eagles' "New Kid in Town."

"He just stopped coming to school one day, and then Lisa Daily told us that he was taken away."

"Geez, Queenie, you can't believe everything Lisa Daily says. Maybe Jimmy Prosciutto just moved."

"Perusitto," she corrects me.

The Eagles fade away and an elevator version of the Beatles' "Day Tripper" takes its place. "Who's Lisa Daily anyway?" I say. "She's just some silly nit with teeth too big for her head. She looks like a demented buck-toothed rabbit." I make a face, sticking my teeth out to prove my point.

Queenie considers this long enough to stop crying and then laughs, despite her fears. She looks at Cid, who makes the same face as me so that we both look like demented rabbits.

"*I'm Lisa Daily,*" I say in a goofy voice, just as the receptionist picks up the line. She's curt and sounds totally fed up.

"Can I help you?"

"Oh . . . hi . . . uhm, yes, I'm calling about my ma."

"Yes?"

"Well, she's really sick and we don't know what to do. We called the doctor's office but they're closed until tomorrow."

"You'll have to bring her in to Emergency if there's a problem."

"We haven't got a car."

"Call a cab," the woman says.

"But she's really sick. She can't get out of bed and she won't eat anything. I don't think she's able to go anywhere. Can't the doctor just make a house call?"

"Doctors don't make house calls," she snips. "This isn't the Old West."

I shake my head at Cid and point at the phone like I can't believe what I'm hearing. "Do you always talk to people so rudely?"

The woman sighs. The edge leaves her voice. I imagine her slumping over her desk in defeat. "Look, sonny, if you think it's necessary, you can use Emergency Services."

"Emergency Services?"

"An ambulance."

"Could you send one over?"

"You have to call 911," she says, and then disconnects the line like I'm some kind of crank caller.

I crash the phone down in its cradle. "What an old bag!"

"What'd she say?" Cid and Queenie ask in unison.

"Call an ambulance." I make the buck-toothed rabbit face again, but neither Cid nor Queenie laughs. Just then, the organ music begins. It drones louder and louder until it feels like the whole house is going to collapse.

"That's it," Cid says. "Ma doesn't need to hear that crap." She jumps up and storms over to the stairs.

"What are you going to do?" Queenie asks.

"I'm going to smash that organ to pieces." Cid marches down the stairs and outside. We hear her bang on the neighbours' door. The organ continues. Cid pounds on the door again, this time louder and angrier.

The organ deflates to a stop. There is a pause and then we hear the door open. Queenie and I rush to listen at the hot-air vent on the floor, placing our ears close to the grille.

"I'm afraid you can't practise your organ today," we hear Cid say.

There is silence from the other party. I can just imagine what she's thinking, seeing some furious punk rocker with white clown hair making demands on her doorstep. We hear Cid murmur something, and then the door creaks to a close and locks, the chain engaged. Cid comes back up the stairs.

"What happened?" I ask.

Cid shrugs. "She just stopped. I didn't have to threaten her or anything. She's just a little kid, maybe nine or ten. She looked scared out of her mind." Cid laughs.

"Do you blame her?" I say.

"I wasn't mean or anything," Cid says. "I simply suggested that she take up a less obnoxious instrument, like the air guitar."

Queenie shuffles off to the bathroom while Cid and I discuss what the hospital receptionist said. Neither of us feels we should call an ambulance at this point. Until Queenie comes back into the room, stunned as a zombie. She holds a pill bottle out in her hand.

"I found this in the garbage."

"What is it?"

She walks toward me, arm outstretched.

Cid snatches the bottle, checks the label and shakes it. It's empty. "Call the ambulance," she says.

"Why?"

"Just call it!" she shouts.

I pick up the phone and dial.

"It's Valium," Cid says, sticking the bottle in my face. "Ma must have taken them."

"All of them?"

"You've reached Emergency Services. How may I direct your call?"

"My ma's sick," I say, stumbling over the words. "She may have taken something—Valium I think."

Queenie bursts into tears again. The dispatcher takes our information and tells me the ambulance will arrive shortly.

In less than five minutes, we can hear the siren wailing as it approaches. The ambulance screeches to a stop in front of the house. From the sun porch window I see two attendants jump out. They're really tall and dressed in matching uniforms. They exchange some bit of lighthearted banter as they produce a stretcher from the back of the truck and carry it up to the house. I open the door before they have a chance to ring the bell. They follow me to Ma's room and set the stretcher down. One of them walks up to Ma's bed. He talks in a clear, loud voice, enunciating every word.

"Mrs. Estabrooks . . . my name is Bobby . . . I'm with the Suffolk County Emergency Medical Services."

Ma opens her eyes briefly and looks confused.

"Have you taken any pills, Mrs. Estabrooks?"

Ma doesn't answer. The man puts his hand on her shoulder and tells her that they are going to take her to Emergency and that everything will be okay. They set up the stretcher and then move Ma from the bed, covering her in a blanket and quickly strapping her in. They seem to really know what they're doing as they manoeuvre skilfully through the narrow hall and down the stairs. They slide Ma into the ambulance. One of the attendants sits in the back with her. The other turns to me.

"Is your father here?"

I shake my head.

"Who's coming to the hospital with us? We have room for one up front."

Cid says, "You go, Nathaniel." She tosses me my sneakers and I jump into the ambulance, stuffing my feet into my shoes as the truck fires up.

"Let's go," the driver calls out.

The engine roars and the radio blares, "Pretty Little Angel Eyes." I look at the driver in shock as though it must be a mistake but he doesn't seem to notice the music at all.

"Make some noise, Bobby," the attendant in the back of the truck shouts as we pull away.

Bobby flips a switch on the console and the siren begins to whine, only to stutter to a stop as soon as it starts. He hammers his fist on the roof of the ambulance until the siren kicks in again, the high-pitched squall and flashing lights drawing people from their homes and cars to watch. Bobby turns to me and smiles.

"She's singing now," he says, like we're on some kind of joyride.

I grip the seat as we careen down the street, cars criss-crossing left and right in front of us, the drivers unsure of what to do. Some pull over, the way they're supposed to, but most just zigzag around until we pass.

"Look at 'em run," Bobby says. He laughs like a hyena. The guy must be bananas. The way he's driving, I won't be surprised if we crash the ambulance and then we'll all be in the hospital—or worse. And poor Ma is stuck in the back! I grip the seat tighter. We turn down Wellington Street, the ambulance taking the corner so sharply I'm sure we're up on two wheels. Bobby tromps on it as we race down the hill toward the hospital, hitting the dip at the bottom of the street and practically ramping the ambulance into the air like the cars in *The Streets of San Francisco*. He slows down just in time to make the turn into the hospital lot, pulling up smoothly to the Emergency entrance. I'm amazed we made it alive. I hope Ma's okay.

Now that we're in front of the hospital, the attendants are all serious and professional again. They get out and lift the stretcher from the ambulance as though it contains rare china. You'd never know they almost killed us just getting here. I trot alongside Ma, to keep up as the attendants enter the hospital and wheel the stretcher past a blur of broken-down people all waiting to see the doctor. I'm struck by the smell of antiseptic and alcohol and sickness. Babies howl at the top of their lungs, and nurses and orderlies bustle around. We go through a set of double doors and the attendants hand off Ma's stretcher to some nurses waiting in the hallway. I try to follow but an orderly guides me in the other direction. He sits me down at the nurses' station.

"The nurse needs you to provide some information," he says in a concerned and caring voice.

The nurse is an older woman with black cat-eye glasses and dyed red hair scraped back in a bun. She reminds me of Nurse Ratched from *One Flew Over the Cuckoo's Nest*. She produces a form attached to a clipboard.

"You're going to have to fill this out," she says, handing me the form and a pen.

Right away, I'm aware that I've forgotten Ma's health card at home. I explain this to Nurse Ratched and her mouth contracts to the size of an asterisk. When I finish filling out the form, I hand it back and she checks it. She's already printed out a bracelet for Ma and punched out a blue hospital admittance card, despite my oversight.

"Husband?" she asks me as she scans the form.

I shake my head.

She makes a note.

"What are they going to do for my ma?" I ask.

"They'll have to pump her stomach. You the oldest?"

I shake my head again. "My sister, Cid. She's fifteen."

"Who should we put down for next of kin?"

"Uh . . . me, I guess."

"No aunts or uncles close by?" she asks.

"No."

She purses her lips again and makes another note on the form. "You can have a seat in the waiting room," she tells me, and goes back to her files.

"How long will it be?" I ask.

"It's hard to say."

I stand there, my head full of questions, but Nurse Ratched has already forgotten me. I turn around and look at the room full of people, all of them impatient and desperate. The babies are still crying. There is a man doubled over in his chair next to a girl with a makeshift bandage around her hand. Several old peo-ple sit in various stages of collapse and a cluster of little kids wanders aimlessly around. I take a seat against the wall so I can see the TV. Immediately, a little kid with a snotty nose comes up to me and waves a dirty stuffed toy in my face. There's a five-alarm smell coming from the kid's diaper and his face is so grubby he looks like he's been eating handfuls of mud. I hold my nose and turn my head, praying the kid will go away.

There's no sound on the TV but it doesn't matter. It's tuned to some baseball game that nobody cares about, and you couldn't hear anyway overtop of the babies. Looking around the room at all the misery and desperation, I feel as though I'm going to cry. I don't know what's going to happen to Ma. I don't know why she would want to take pills and make herself sick. I blame myself and Dad, cursing him in my heart. He left us, and now Ma's unstable—even worse than Charlie Chaplin's mother. At least *she* didn't try to kill herself. I image all sorts of things—awful things that I don't want to think about, but my mind won't stop churning.

As I blink back the tears, my eyes meet those of an old woman sitting across the room. Her face is creased like a worn cotton shirt but I can see that she's kind. Her eyes seem to shine as though there's a little light burning inside her, and I wonder why I didn't notice her before. We stare at each other. It's as if she can see right to the heart of me. She smiles, nodding gently, easing my panic. But then a baby shrieks and I break my gaze. When I look back, the old woman is gone. I scan the room. She's nowhere in sight. Maybe she went to the washroom. I see a couple of vending machines against the wall, one for coffee and the other for chocolate bars and chips. I check my pants pockets for change but come back with a handful of lint. It's going to be a long night.

chapter 11
I lose hope

I've been sitting in the waiting room for nearly three hours, monitoring the rhythms of the Emergency ward. Most of the cases coming in don't seem like emergencies at all: coughs and pains that seem to clear up on their own as soon as a prescription is written, twisted ankles and sore knees that just need a bit of ice or rest. I can't believe people actually choose to come to the hospital instead of dealing with these things themselves. It's like torture to have to be here.

In the hours that I've been waiting, I've travelled through every possible emotion, from hope to despair, to anger and sorrow and back again, the music from the ambulance looping endlessly through my head. I can't believe that Ma would do something that would endanger her life. I can't believe that she would rather die and leave us behind than go on and face things. I feel so sad, so guilty and sorry about everything. I wish Queenie and Cid were here. I miss Smokey like crazy and think about walking to the barn just to see him. In the hours I've spent waiting here, I could have been there and back several times. I don't know why it's taking so long and I think I'm going to freak out if something doesn't happen soon.

As the night ticks away, more people leave than arrive, until there's just me and a couple other people. The crying babies are gone, thankfully, and the kid with the smelly diaper too. Bobby the psychotic ambulance driver and his sidekick show up with another patient on a stretcher. It's an old man, his face pinched with pain—probably from the crazy ambulance ride he had to endure rather than some ailment he's facing. But that's pretty much it. The Emergency ward seems to be slowing down for the night. I check Dad's watch. It's 9:30.

By 9:45, I'm so upset and uncomfortable from sitting around waiting that I finally risk talking to Nurse Ratched. I approach her desk.

"Excuse me . . ."

She doesn't look up.

"Excuse me . . . when can I see my mother?"

She continues to type as though I don't exist, then finally flips through some sheets on another clipboard and scans the rows of entries.

"It's Estabrooks," I say, to help her along.

"The patient has been admitted to room 317."

"What? Why didn't they tell me?" I don't even thank her, I just head for the elevators. I follow the signs on the walls, and as I'm coming around the corner I run smack into Cid and Queenie, coming from the other direction.

"Hey! What are you doing here?"

They both seem totally relieved to see me. Cid is wearing my old Toronto Maple Leafs cap over her crazy hair. Queenie is a mess, wearing a faded Bugs Bunny T-shirt and a worn pair of sweatpants. The laces on her sneakers are undone. How did she get so dishevelled?

"We couldn't wait any longer," she says.

"We want to know what's going on with Ma," Cid says. "Where is she? Is she all right?"

"I don't know. They haven't told me anything. I was just going up to see her now. She's in room 317."

Queenie spins toward the elevators. I grab her by the back of the shirt. "Hang on," I say. "Tie up your sneakers and fix your hair. We don't want Ma to worry. And why are you wearing these old clothes when Ma bought you new ones?"

Queenie shrugs. Cid quickly combs through Queenie's hair with her fingers, plaiting it into a thick, neat braid and securing it with a rubber band from her pants pocket. When Cid is done, Queenie laces up her sneakers. She turns to me for approval and I nod. She looks much better now.

We bustle mutely along the corridor to the elevators,

past the darkened tuck shop closed for the night, past the visitors' reception booth where a sole volunteer is installed, reading a book beneath the glow of a lamp. The hospital has a sombre hush over it like a library, every noise sounding amplified and hollow. I engage the elevator and we wait for it to arrive. The light finally blinks off, the door opening with a mechanical *ding*. We get inside and push the button for the third floor. Just as the door is closing, an orderly rattles toward us with a cart. I press the "open" button to be polite, causing the doors to jump back with a *clunk*. We have to squeeze against the walls to make room.

"What floor?" I ask.

"Five," he says, smiling as he assesses our motley crew.

The door closes and the elevator slowly begins to ascend. The orderly glances at us again, then checks his watch. He must be wondering what three kids are doing in the hospital so late. We reach the third floor at last and shuffle out, leaving the orderly to ride the elevator on his own.

The third floor is dimly lit, the low light casting shadows like dark spectres along the hall. The air is close and stale with the smell of disinfectant and medicines and sorrow, and we can hear an odd breathing sound, like the rise and fall of a hesitant piston, punctuated by little clicks and beeps. About halfway down the corridor shines a beacon of light, illuminating the nurses' station. We talk in whispers as we walk in a huddle, past the cheerless doorways of the patients' rooms, checking numbers as we go. From somewhere down the hall someone moans. Queenie and Cid look at me with frightened faces. We're like the characters from *The Wizard of Oz*, moving through the haunted forest, trying to muster our courage—until a voice causes us to jump with fear.

"May I help you?"

It's the nurse at the station. We couldn't see her sitting behind the high white counter. "We're looking for Mrs. Estabrooks," I say.

"It's long past visiting hours," the nurse says, not unkindly. She's a lot younger than Nurse Ratched and she isn't nearly as intimidating. She actually looks kind of pretty and nice, with her dark eyes and her brown hair in a ponytail.

"But we need to see our ma," Queenie says, her voice quaking. "She's been here so long and we don't know what's wrong with her."

The nurse checks her files. "Estabrooks. Room 317. That's two doors down on the right." She looks up at us and smiles. "Go on in. But one at a time. We don't want to overwhelm."

I point to my stomach. "Did they . . .?"

She checks the files again and shakes her head. "They found nothing," she says. "No traces of Valium or medications of any kind, except for a small amount of aspirin."

Cid and I sigh with relief. I feel immediately guilty for thinking what I'd thought about Ma.

"She didn't take any pills," the nurse clarifies. "We were mistaken."

"What's wrong with her then?" Cid asks.

"We're not sure at this time. We've done some preliminary tests, but nothing conclusive. She has some fluid in her lungs."

"What does that mean?" I ask.

The nurse thinks for a moment. "Could be a number of things. We can't say until the test results come back. But my guess is pneumonia."

"Pneumonia? Is that bad?" I ask.

"It can be."

We all just stand there. None of us knows what to say. It's all so serious and real that it doesn't feel real at all. It's like a bad dream, only we're all in it together. The nurse must sense our confusion because she gets up from her chair and offers to show us the way. We follow her gratefully down the hall and wait as she peeks into Ma's room.

"Margaret," she calls out softly.

It sounds strange to hear Ma's name like that.

"Margaret," she calls again, then disappears into Ma's room. She comes back a moment later and indicates for me to go in, but catches me at the door. "We've given her something to help her sleep. She probably won't know you're here, but you can sit by the bed."

I step into the room and let my eyes adjust. The curtains are drawn and the lights are off, save for a tiny one above the bed. I see Ma, tucked neatly under the sheets. She's hooked up to an IV with several bags of clear fluid dripping into a tube that leads to her arm. Her dark hair is loose and flowing across the pillow, and she looks as serene as an angel surrounded by so much white. I creep across the room. There's another clipboard with charts and scribbled notes on a hook at the foot of the bed. I study it to see if I can make sense of the chart but it's just an indecipherable jumble to me. I feel clumsy and awkward and out of place, standing over Ma like this. "Get better, Ma" is all I can think to whisper before I turn around and leave the room.

Back in the hall, I convince the nurse to let Cid and Queenie go in together. I don't want Queenie alone in there with Ma. It was scary enough for me on my own. Queenie and Cid disappear into the room. I'm just about to ask the nurse what the charts on the clipboard mean when I hear Queenie burst into tears. I rush back in.

"Poor Ma!" she sobs, as she collapses in a heap against Cid, who catches her and ushers her from the room. Cid is crying now too, guiding Queenie to the station, where the nurse sits her down and hands her a tissue. She passes the box to Cid, who yanks out several tissues and blows her nose loudly. She sounds like Stan Laurel from Laurel and Hardy, which would be funny if it weren't for the circumstances.

"It's still early," the nurse reassures us. "She's resting comfortably now. We should know more in the morning." She checks her watch and sees that it's very late. "Can I call someone to come pick you up . . . your father . . .?"

"We're taking a cab home," I say, knowing full well I haven't got any money.

"Let me call one for you," she offers.

"No, we don't want to trouble you. There's a direct line down in the lobby." I give Queenie and Cid a look to let them know that we should go now. It passes right over Queenie's head but Cid catches it and takes Queenie's hand.

"Thanks for all your help," I say.

The nurse smiles brightly. "Visiting hours are from 8:00 a.m. till 8:00 p.m."

I give her a little wave as we leave.

"Do we have money for a cab?" Cid asks when we reach the lobby.

"I didn't even have money for a coffee from the vending machine," I confess. "But it's a nice night out," I add as we pass through the sliding glass doors to the street.

None of us speak for several blocks. For some reason, I can't get the image of the old woman's face out of my head.

"There was an old woman in the waiting room," I say.

Cid looks at me, expecting me to explain. "And?"

"I don't know. There was something different about her . . . the way she looked at me."

"What do you mean?"

"Like she knew me or something."

"Maybe she's from your paper route."

"No . . . I've never seen her before. It was weird."

"Because she looked at you?"

"No . . . it was like she had this light around her. Like an angel or something."

"That is weird."

"Forget it," I say. The whole thing seems stupid when I try to explain it. Cid's lost interest already. Queenie sniffles and snuffles beside me, a little dip in her walk. I think she's going to start dancing but then she turns to me dolefully. "I'm hungry," she says.

"Me too," Cid agrees.

"Yeah, me three," I say. "Did you guys eat dinner?"

Queenie shakes her head. "We were waiting to hear from you and Ma. Besides, I didn't feel hungry until now. My stomach was full of flies."

"Butterflies," Cid corrects her.

"No," Queenie says. "I've had butterflies before and they don't feel like that. These were just flies."

I have to laugh at this. "Well, we can make something when we get home."

It only takes about half an hour for us to walk home, and even though it's just a crummy apartment, it still feels good to get there after being at the hospital so long. Then I think of Ma, stuck in some strange bed, hooked up to an IV tube, and I feel wretched again. She'll be scared and lonely when she wakes up. I have to shake this thought from my mind because I don't want Queenie to pick up on my mood.

"What do you want to eat?" I ask.

"KD," Queenie says.

"We've eaten KD three times this week," Cid complains.

I frown and she quickly changes tack. "Okay," she says, "but we get to put tuna and peas in it this time."

Queenie doesn't mind. She even gets the cans of tuna and peas from the cupboard and opens them while Cid puts the water on to boil. The macaroni is ready in no time and soon we're scraping our plates with our forks. I didn't even realize how hungry I was.

Queenie yawns and gets up from the table, placing her dish in the sink. She drags herself to the living room and flops onto the couch. Cid watches her, then turns to me, speaking in a low voice.

"I'm worried," she says.

"Yeah, me too."

She shakes her head, leaning back in her chair to check on Queenie, who's already snoring lightly, one arm dangling over the edge of the couch.

"Not just about Ma. I'm worried over what Queenie said . . . about the Children's Aid."

"Why?"

"Think about it," she says. "What if Ma doesn't get better? What if something awful really does happen?"

"Don't even talk that way, Cid."

"We have to talk about it," she insists. "What if something happens and Ma isn't here to take care of us? What will we do? Where will we go? We don't have anyone to turn to." She pushes her fork across her plate, plowing tiny field rows through the leftover cheese sauce. She plows row after row, and I can tell she's preparing to drop a bomb. "Dad left us, and we have no idea how to find him."

"But we'll be okay," I say.

Cid looks at me like I'm completely naive. "As much as I would like to believe that, it isn't true and you know it, Nathaniel. It's not like we've got tons of money or anything. And neither of us is considered an adult in the eyes of the law. We don't have any relatives to go to. Dad's brother is long gone. Ma has nobody. And even if there is some relative somewhere, no one would be willing to take all three of us together. We're screwed." She pushes herself from the table and clatters her plate into the sink.

She leaves the kitchen and I hear the door to the apartment open and close.

I sit there, Cid's words clanging around in my head, until I can't stand it any more and I get up to go look for her. Before I go downstairs, though, I adjust the fan on the floor so it's not blowing right in Queenie's face. She's sleeping so peacefully, I don't want to wake her just to tell her to go to bed.

I find Cid on the stairs at the front of the house, smoking. She's sitting with her back all stiff and straight, the way Ma does when she's worried about things.

She doesn't look at me but holds the pack up, offering me a smoke.

"No . . . no thanks."

"Queenie's asleep. She won't know."

"I just don't feel like it is all."

I sit down next to her and look out over the park. The trees are standing at attention along the perimeter, like dark soldiers awaiting orders in the shadows. The plumes of blue smoke from Cid's cigar drift slowly in the humid night air.

"Where do you think Dad is?" I say.

Cid pulls my Leafs cap from her head and hangs it over her knee, fluffing up her mop with one hand. She takes another draw on the cigar and contemplates the question.

"Back in the States."

"In Illinois?"

"That would be my guess."

"Do you think there's any way to find him?"

"I don't know." She puffs thoughtfully on her cigar. "I tried to call him once," she confesses. "But I couldn't find his number. It's either unlisted or he doesn't have a phone, because the operator came up empty."

It surprises me to hear that Cid tried to call Dad. "Do you think he's in Brookfield?"

Cid shrugs and continues to smoke while I poke at a scab on my leg, choosing my words carefully so she knows that I'm in earnest. "We'll make it through somehow, Cid. You don't have to worry. I can get a job—a real job, enough to pay the rent and buy groceries so we can get by."

Cid shakes her head, blowing smoke forcefully between pursed lips. "You're thirteen, Nathaniel. What kind of job do you really think you can get?"

"I don't know. Something. I'll do whatever I have to so that we can stay together."

She shakes her head again but her eyes soften and she lets her back relax. We sit on the stairs, wrestling with our thoughts. I try to imagine what it would be like to live without Ma and Queenie and Cid. I think about the Children's Aid coming to take us away and breaking us apart so that we'll never see one another again. I imagine them coming to take Smokey as well, and selling him to some kid who belongs to a fancy pony club. My mind skips over all the possibilities of what might be and I decide then and there that I will never let any of it happen, no matter what.

chapter 12
out of the frying pan . . .

The next morning we're all up at the crack of dawn. None of us could sleep. We gather in the kitchen to discuss what we should do. I encourage Cid and Queenie to go to the barn to take care of Smokey while I go to the hospital to check on Ma. I convince them that the hospital won't let us all in at once to visit Ma anyway, so there's no point in the three of us going at the same time. Secretly, I'd rather be the one to sneak away to the stable for a ride today. Even cleaning out stalls would be better than going to the hospital. But we've decided to take turns to make it easier on everyone. I have to call old McKinley again, to let him know that Ma is in the hospital and won't be in to work for a while. I hope McKinley understands and that Ma won't lose her job.

Once we've agreed on what to do we fall silent over our cereal. I'm the first one to push away from the table, placing my dishes in the sink next to the pile that has accumulated since Ma got sick. The sight of the dirty dishes makes me sad. Ma never leaves the house in a mess.

"We have to do the dishes and keep the place clean," I say. "We don't want Ma coming home to a hovel."

McKinley seems genuinely concerned when I tell him that Ma is in the hospital. To my relief, he says to tell Ma not to worry about work and to just get better. After I hang up the phone, I prepare to go. By eight o'clock, I'm dressed and out the door, leaving Cid and Queenie behind to go tend to Smokey. I know Cid swore she'd never go to the new barn again, but, given the circumstances, she'll have to swallow her pride, because Queenie can't go alone.

I'm walking to the hospital as quickly as I can, fifteen dollars in change jingling in my pocket from my cigar box savings. I don't want to spend another day at that place without food or something to drink.

I take a shortcut through the park. The morning is sunny and bright, the birds singing cheerfully. At the homes around the park, people are already up, watering their lawns and puttering in their gardens. It's Tuesday morning and everything is rolling along as always. You'd never know there was any trouble in the world from the looks of it. I wonder if Ma is up, reading or enjoying breakfast. I try to imagine her like that, feeling better and on the mend, but I can't stop my mind from slipping into some very dark corners all the same. I'm so tangled up in my thoughts that, before

I know it, I'm standing in front of the elevators at the hospital, pushing the button. The panic starts to rise up in me again because I have no idea what to expect when I reach Ma's room.

The third floor isn't nearly as intimidating in the daylight as it was at night. There's the same awful smell as before, only now there are several old people parked in wheelchairs at strategic locations along the hall. One old man looks up cheerfully when he sees me arrive, as though he's been expecting me. He hasn't a tooth in his head but he smiles broadly, his pink gums flashing.

"Tommy!" he says, like I'm his long-lost son.

I smile politely and walk past, but the old man chases after me in his wheelchair with astonishing speed and grabs me by the pant leg.

"Where are the showgirls?" he demands.

I stand there awkwardly, not knowing what to do. "My name's Nathaniel," I say.

The old man looks at me more closely and screws up his face. "What have you done with Eileen?"

"I'm sorry . . . I don't know any Eileen . . . my name is Nathaniel . . . I'm here to see my ma."

His face sharpens and I think he's going to start yelling at me, when one of the nurses comes to my aid.

"Now, Mr. Corruthers . . ." she scolds as she wheels the old man back to his position by the elevators.

I walk quickly down the hall to Ma's room. But when I go inside, she's not there.

"The tests for pneumonia came back positive," the nurse informs me. "Your mother has been moved to the ICU."

I stare back at her in confusion.

"Intensive Care Unit—sixth floor," she says.

I run down the hall, practically knocking Mr. Corruthers from his wheelchair when he tries to stop me in front of the stairs. I've got no time to wait for the elevators. Taking the steps two at a time, I burst onto the sixth floor. The Intensive Care Unit is lit up like the bridge of the Starship *Enterprise*. It's all glass and gleaming floors, with the rooms in a circle around the nurses' station for easy monitoring. I can't see Ma at first. All the patients look the same. I stand in the centre of the room until the nurse notices me. When I tell her who I am, she points at a room to her left.

"The fluid in her lungs has gotten worse," she says. "She's heavily sedated."

Her voice sounds distant and small to my ears, as though she's coming in over the radio. She hands me a mask, gloves and a gown. My heart pounding, I fumble to put them on.

Ma is lying under clean white sheets, the same as before. Her arms are yellowed with bruises where the nurses have taken blood and her face has a funny expression. It's all slack, and her eyes are partially open, moving back and forth beneath half-closed lids. At first I think she's awake, but then I understand that she is very deep in sleep. I pull up a chair and sit on the edge, watching.

After fifteen minutes, I lean over and check the chart at the end of the bed. There are more papers and more scribbles but still nothing that means anything to me. I look around the room. It's stark and bare. I'm so stunned with fear, so scared and disbelieving that all I can think about is how I should have brought flowers to brighten things up. I drift from the room to talk to the nurse.

She's very kind and helpful, offering me lots of information, like that one in a hundred people get pneumonia every year, and that there are several different kinds. It can come on really quickly, she says, and usually it's just like a bad cold, but sometimes it's fatal. She regrets this last part, trying to take back her words as I look at her, unable to hide the despair that takes over me. I feel like Queenie, asking all kinds of questions that no one could possibly answer, like, Is Ma in any pain? When will she be able to come home? And, How did it happen? She tries as best she can to answer me, talking about viruses and bacteria and things.

"Your mom didn't want to get sick," she comforts me. "It just happened."

I say nothing, even though I'm grateful for what the nurse is trying to do. She wants me to know that Ma got sick, plain and simple, and that it wasn't from taking the pills that Queenie found. Ma didn't give up on us. She just wasn't strong enough to stay well.

I turn to go back to Ma's room but decide to go down to the tuck shop and purchase some flowers instead. I hope they have daisies. They're Ma's favourites. I drop the mask and gloves in the garbage then place the gown in the dirty laundry bin in the hall. I tell the nurse that I'll be back. I take the stairs again instead of the elevator, because I feel all claustrophobic and crazy.

As soon as I walk into the tuck shop I can see that they don't have bouquets of daisies. All they have are expensive arrangements of flowers pushed into green Styrofoam. The cheapest is a small vase of dahlias for $13.50. The tax eats up the rest of my lunch money and I'm broke again. I don't care, really. I almost never eat lunch anyway. A book of crosswords would have been nice, though. The woman asks if I need the flowers wrapped but I tell her no. She sees me hovering over the crosswords.

"Pick one," she says.

"I don't have any money left."

"It's on the house."

I pick a book with a bright purple cover and she nods with approval, then slides a little card across the counter toward me. It's no bigger than a couple of postage stamps and has a picture of a rose in the top left corner.

"It comes with the flowers," she says. "You can sign it so they know who the gift is from." She smiles and hands me a pen.

I stare at the card, wondering what to write.

"Most people just say something like 'Get well soon,'" the woman kindly says.

I write the words, then sign the card from me, Cid and Queenie. Somehow, it doesn't seem like enough. But I return the pen and card to the woman and she inserts the card into a holder that looks like a clear plastic fork. She places it among the dahlias and hands the flowers to me.

"Good luck," she says.

The nurse stops me at the door when I go to deliver my gift to Ma. Flowers are not allowed in ICU rooms for sanitary reasons, she gently explains. She says that I can put them on the counter of the nurses' station, next to the others that just arrived. She points to a small bouquet of white carnations in a little vase, with baby's breath and tiny pink roses. I check the card on the carnations and I'm shocked to see Mr. McKinley's name beneath the words "Get well soon." I guess he's not so bad, sending Ma flowers, though I wish he'd spent a little more money for something bigger. And I don't want my card and Mr. McKinley's card to say the same thing. I ask the nurse for a pen and write "We love you, Ma" on the back of my card, then reinsert it into the holder. I place the dahlias on the counter, next to McKinley's carnations. In the bright glare of the lights, the flowers look small and insignificant.

"We'll let your mom know the flowers are here when she wakes up," the nurse says.

I thank her, then sit outside Ma's room, staring at a crossword but unable to think. Glancing in at Ma from time to time, I can't bring myself to really look at her. It's just too painful to see her like that. Eventually I manage to doze off, the book balanced on my lap, a pencil in hand. I sleep until another nurse bustles in to check the IV and perform her duties. She unlocks the wheels on Ma's bed and begins to roll her from the room.

"X-rays," she says, answering my unspoken question.

I play absently with the pages of the crossword book until Ma and the nurse reappear. Ma's eyes flutter open and brighten with recognition when she sees me. She struggles to sit up.

"Nathaniel . . ."

I rush to her side but the nurse stops me.

"You have to wear protection," she says.

Ma has fallen asleep again by the time I'm suited up. I feel like a doctor with the gown and gloves and mask. I take Ma's hand in mine. She stirs, looking up into my eyes. I hope she can tell that I'm smiling at her behind the mask.

"I'm sorry," she whispers.

I blink back the tears. I don't want Ma to see me cry. "I love you, Ma . . ." I can't stop my voice from breaking.

Ma's eyes close. I stand helplessly next to the bed until the doctor comes into the room. He nods at me then frowns over the charts. When he's done, the nurse tells him that I'm Ma's son. He meets me in the hallway, pulling his mask down below his chin. I do the same.

"It looks serious," he tells me, man to man. "But your mother is still young. She has a lot of fight in her."

"When will she be better?" I say, trying to keep my cool. I don't want him to think that I'm just a kid.

"That's up to your mom . . . and the Big Guy," he says, pointing upward. "We're doing everything we can down here. You've got my word on that." He shakes my hand and goes to tend his next patient.

"That's Dr. Weisner," the nurse tells me. "He's a very good doctor."

I remove the gloves, mask and gown as I thank her and take my seat outside Ma's room. The rest of the day is uneventful, with me just sitting and dozing and Ma lost in her dream world. I haven't got the heart to do the crosswords. At one point the nurse brings me a carton of milk. She shows me where the kitchen is and tells me that I am welcome to use the fridge, or make tea or coffee if I like. I sit in my seat for the rest of the day, the carton of milk growing warm in my hands as the sun slips slowly from the sky.

* * *

Cid and Queenie are waiting for me when I get home. They grill me about Ma. I'm so hungry I can barely get a sentence out. I scarf some bread straight from the bag. I don't even toast it or spread jelly on. They pepper me with questions as I stuff my face. Now I know how the nurses must feel. The whole time I'm eating I'm thinking about what I should actually tell Queenie and Cid. I have no intention of worrying Queenie with the truth. I decide to tell them that the doctors think Ma has a really bad cold. I don't mention that the tests came back positive for pneumonia, or how the nurse said it can be fatal. The girls ask dozens of questions, faster than I can answer. I finally interrupt the barrage to ask after Smokey. I've had enough hospital talk for one day.

"Look at my new boots!" Queenie blurts out. She stands and pulls up her jeans. She's wearing a beautiful pair of real leather English riding boots that must have cost a fortune. "Alyson gave them to me!"

I look at Cid, who gives me a shrug.

"She's *sooo* nice!" Queenie raves. "She said that I can keep them and that they used to be hers when she was my age."

She struts around the kitchen for a bit, showing off the boots and talking a blue streak. "I introduced Alyson to Cid and she was really nice to Cid, too. She said that she'll teach Cid how to ride properly if Cid wants, and that Cid can even take a turn on her horse, Ben. She's not at all like the other girls—is she, Cid?"

Cid gives a little hum of agreement then rolls her eyes at me behind Queenie's back.

"Oh, and you know what else she told me?" Queenie says in a voice like she just cracked the Caramilk secret. "She used to have a problem with her leg when she was even younger than me, so her parents got her into riding to help her coordination and to strengthen her muscles so she wouldn't limp. She's all better now but she used to wear a brace on her leg and everything. Isn't that neat?"

Now I understand why Alyson is so nice to Queenie. I just assumed that she was a privileged little princess who hadn't a care in the world. The idea of her struggling with a leg brace as a little child immediately changes my opinion of her. My face flushes with shame when I remember the way I treated her.

"She taught me lots of really good things today," Queenie continues, "like how to canter around the ring at an even pace without disturbing the other riders, and how to control the horse using your feet instead of the reins. Alyson says that I'm a natural and that if I try hard, I can compete with the Eastview Pony Club at the Equestrian Games. She even said that I have a good chance of winning something! Isn't that amazing?"

Queenie jumps up and down and claps her hands, her face shining with joy. I look at Cid for confirmation. She nods.

"She's really good," Cid admits. "She's better than both of us."

"And what did you do the whole time Queenie was riding?" I ask.

Cid makes a motion like she's mucking out a stall. "I kept to myself," she says.

I laugh because it's exactly what I would have done. I can tell that Cid is trying to make an effort to be okay about the stable and Alyson and everything else, what with Ma being sick and all. I'm really proud of her for putting her anger and grievances aside.

Queenie pipes up again, telling how she and Cid rode Smokey in the field after her riding lesson, and that Cid invented a cowboy game where they used a rope to lasso fence posts as though they were working cattle.

"It's okay to relax a bit doing things like that after working hard at a lesson," Queenie says, no doubt quoting Alyson.

Cid rolls her eyes again, but I'm sure she doesn't hold it against Queenie for acting like a know-it-all. She's probably happy that Queenie was able to have some fun and forget about our troubles for a while. I know I am. I wish that I'd been able to spend the day roping fence posts instead of sitting in the hospital. But it's not Ma's fault that she's sick.

I push what's left of the bread to one side. "What do you want for dinner?" I ask.

We make tomato soup and toast with butter for supper, staying up late to watch *Creature Features* because none of us wants to go to bed. Queenie falls asleep on the couch again, still wearing her new riding boots despite the heat in the house.

When I'm sure that Queenie is sound asleep, I decide to tell Cid what's really going on with Ma. "I have to tell you something," I say in a whisper. She looks at me, the fear visible in her eyes. She's scared and so am I, but she has to know the truth. I explain what the nurse told me, about Ma having pneumonia, and how it's fatal some-times. I tell her that Queenie doesn't need to know and that we should be prepared for anything. Cid seems to understand what this means, though I'm not even sure what I'm getting at. We sit on the floor, the fan whirling at our feet, the sound on the TV turned down so low we can barely hear it. We just sit there, saying nothing, drowsiness creeping up on us, until we both eventually fall asleep right there.

* * *

The next day is a blur. I go to the barn to take care of Smokey, while Cid and Queenie see Ma. I ride Smokey to the back field and try roping some fence posts the way the girls did, but I can't find any joy in it. Smokey seems to understand that something is up, as well. From the moment he sees me, he doesn't whinny or stamp his feet. Instead, he tickles my arm with his muz-zle and rubs his head against my chest. He's quiet and not at all frisky as I brush him and saddle him and lead him from the barn to the field. Once there, he stands perfectly still as I mount, and we follow the fenceline, the green pasture rolling out in front of us beneath the blue dome of sky. I urge Smokey to the middle of the field, the grasshoppers jumping and popping in waves before us as we get along. At the top of a small hill, we stop to survey the land. Tree swallows fly all around us, catching insects, their feathers glinting like blue tinfoil in the sun. They swoop and dive, skimming the grass then soaring up to the clouds. I say a prayer for Ma as I watch them, that they might carry my words to heaven on their quick wings.

* * *

I don't spend as much time at the barn as I thought I would. I'm so worried about Ma that I can't enjoy myself. I end up hurrying through things to get back home. Now it's me anxiously waiting to hear news from Queenie and Cid. When I hear the key turn in the lock on the front door, I rush to the top of the stairs.

"Why can't they do anything to help her?" Cid says, her eyes swollen from crying.

I gesture toward Queenie but Cid shakes her head like it's no use trying to hide the truth. Queenie has an absent look on her face. She walks past me to go dance in her bedroom.

"It's 1978!" Cid rages. "They can put a man on the moon but they can't cure pneumonia. It's so stupid!" She kicks a pillow that's lying on the living-room floor then collapses onto the couch, covering her face with her hands.

* * *

The next day at the hospital, I come up to Ma's room in time to hear two of the nurses talking in the hall.

"Hasn't got a snowball's chance in hell," I hear one say to a funny little man in a rumpled brown suit.

The man is carrying a briefcase that matches his attire. He has a moustache just like Charlie Chaplin's. All he needs is a bowler hat and cane to complete the look. The nurse startles when she sees me, then recovers with a smile. It doesn't take me long to figure out that she must have been talking about Ma. She pulls me aside to tell me they've changed Ma's medication, though it's just a shot in the dark at this point. I stare at Ma through the glass. It's not going to be a good day.

★ ★ ★

When I come home, I find Cid and Queenie arguing over something. They're both shrieking and shouting at the top of their lungs. It sounds like they're killing each other, and I can only guess that they're fighting over something to do with Ma. I storm up the stairs and they stop abruptly when they see me.

"What's going on?" I demand.

Queenie whimpers. Cid folds her arms and fumes. "Queenie used the last of the milk to make Hideous J. again. I'm so sick of it, I could scream."

I look at them like they're totally nuts. "What is Hideous J.?"

"Hideous J. Fideous," Queenie says. "That's what she calls KD." She points an accusatory finger at Cid.

"Kraft Dinner? You've got to be kidding me. Don't we have enough to worry about without killing each other over macaroni and cheese? What would Ma say?"

"Ahhh! A centipede!" Queenie shouts.

The bug streaks across the carpet but I jump on it before it can dash under the couch. I stomp on it over and over until it's practically powder. Then I shoot Queenie and Cid a look so poisonous they hang their heads like scolded dogs.

"Mr. McKinley called," Cid mumbles. "He wanted to know how things are."

I don't even answer. I'm so mad at them for fighting over nothing that I don't tell them what I heard the nurse say, or about the man who was in Ma's room. I just go to my own room and slam the door. It's hot from the sun beating in, even with the curtains over the windows. I jump on my bed and lie there for a while, listening to the sputtering drone of a gas lawn mower from somewhere down the street. It's so sweltering in my room that I get up and open a couple of windows to try to cool things down. The old geezer is at his post, staring back at me. I pull the curtain aside to give him the finger and notice someone coming up the walk.

It's the man from the hospital.

chapter 13
the rumpled man

"Someone's coming up the walk!" I shout to Queenie and Cid.

They pile into my room and we crowd around the window, watching. The man steps gingerly up the stairs and we hear him ring the bell on the door. It's one of those old-fashioned, manual bells that you turn instead of press. He rings the bell again, this time more urgently. Nobody moves. This is even scarier than when we used to hide from Clem in the hayloft. Clem lived like an animal in the barn behind the stone house that we rented when we first moved to Canada. He used to chase us with a bullwhip to keep us from playing in the hay. We were terrified of him, because we knew he would use the whip if he caught us. But he never did catch us, because we were too fast and too little, slipping through the hay bales and out between the missing slats of the barn before he could grab us.

"He was at the hospital," I whisper.

"Who?" Cid says.

"That man. He was in Ma's room today, talking to the nurse."

"Why?"

"I don't know, but I don't trust him."

"Why not?"

I shake my head. "He looks like Charlie Chaplin."

Cid scowls. "So what?"

"Why would he be talking to the nurses?" I say.

The bell rings again.

"He's from the Children's Aid," Queenie says.

"He is not," Cid hisses.

"How do you know?" I ask.

"Charlie Chaplin doesn't work for the Children's Aid. He's dead."

"Maybe they like the fact that he *looks* like Charlie Chaplin," I say. "Maybe they think kids will trust him because he's funny and no one suspects him."

"Like the Pied Piper," Queenie whispers. "Or the Child Catcher from Chitty Chitty Bang Bang." She clicks her fingers together and sings in a soft high voice. *"Children . . . ice cream, lollipops . . . all free today . . ."*

"Stop it!" Cid says. She sounds really frightened.

There is a loud pounding on the door. Queenie covers her mouth with her hand. We wait, holding our breath, as though Death himself has come calling. At last, the rumpled man gets fed up and leaves. We watch as he crosses the street to the park. When he reaches the sidewalk, he stops, turns, and squints up at the sun porch. We duck down like criminals, hiding until we think it's safe. After a minute or two, we peek over the windowsill. The rumpled man has moved on, walking at a brisk pace past the jailhouse toward town.

When I stand up, I see that the old man next door is still staring at us from his window. "Get lost!" I shout.

"Ma was right!" Cid says, yanking the curtain closed.

We stay up way past midnight, talking about the rumpled man and why he came. I make jokes, to get the girls laughing, because we're all scared as anything. I say that he was probably selling Avon, or that he was Charlie Chaplin's ghost, searching desperately for his stolen coffin. But in our hearts we fear that he really is from the Children's Aid, and that if Ma doesn't get better soon it's only a matter of time before they cart us away. We talk in circles for hours, the heat in the house stifling, the fan on the living room floor offering little comfort.

Queenie falls asleep in her riding boots, and then Cid fades out too. I lie on the floor beside them, thinking, too confused and anxious to go to bed.

★ ★ ★

The next morning I get up early to go to the barn, and run smack into the rumpled man as I'm leaving the house. I try to dodge back through the door but he catches me, calling out my name before I can slip inside. He trots up the walk, one hand extended. He's wearing the same bad suit as yesterday and his pale skin is flushed red from exerting himself.

"My name is Charlie," he says, taking my hand and shaking it a little too vigorously.

I look at him in disbelief. He's got to be putting me on. "Like the actor," I say, pointing under my nose.

He grins with pride, as though I'm the first person to make this connection. He continues shaking my hand until I look down and he realizes what he's doing and lets go. With a little flourish, he pulls a business card from his breast pocket. "I'm from the Children's Aid Society."

I just about choke when he says this. I pretend to study the card, though I can barely see for the blood pounding in my head.

"Do you mind if I come in?" he asks, stepping up the stairs.

I block his way. "Anyone can print a business card," I say.

This amuses him. He smoothes his moustache with one finger. "We can talk on the steps if you like. I just thought you'd prefer to speak in private." He casts his gaze upward, to where the old man is standing in his front window. I look up too, and notice Queenie and Cid huddled in one of the sun porch windows, watching.

"Got any more ID?" I ask.

The rumpled man pops open his briefcase and pulls out some papers. At the very top of the pile is an official-looking form with the Children's Aid logo in dark ink—and my name typed in bold underneath. I feel like I'm going to be sick.

"You can come in for a bit," I say, trying to sound casual. "But I have to take care of my pony, so I don't have a lot of time."

He snaps his briefcase shut with a practised smile and follows me up the stairs. Queenie and Cid are still hiding in my room when we come in. I wave them over. They shuffle behind us at a distance. I show the man to the table and indicate that he may sit down. He does so with seeming pleasure, as though we're just about to have a good cup of tea.

"This is Charlie," I announce to Queenie and Cid. "He's from the Children's Aid."

"Hello," Charlie says.

The girls stare mutely from the doorway. Charlie seems unfazed.

"Might I have a glass of water?" he asks.

I run the tap and get him a glass, setting it down in front of him. But he doesn't take a sip. Instead he snaps the locks open on his briefcase as if he's about to perform a magic trick. I hover to one side of the table. The man produces several documents, including the one with my name, and arranges them neatly. He turns to me and assumes a pose that he has no doubt rehearsed in front of the mirror a thousand times.

"We want you to know that you are not alone," he launches in. "There is help for dependents in cases like yours. We are aware of your situation, and let me assure you, should something happen to your mother, there are measures in place to safeguard your well-being."

"Like what?" Cid says, coming to life. She steps into the kitchen, her eyes flashing. "How dare you come into our house and talk about our mother."

The smile slides from the man's face. He composes himself quickly, however, folding his hands together on the table as he adopts a look of eternal patience. "I understand your concern—"

"No you don't!" Cid cuts him off. "You don't understand anything. Our mother isn't even dead and you're here butting into our lives, and we're supposed to be grateful for it? You make me sick!"

The man blinks back at her, his lips tightening, his

face clouding with anger. He speaks in a controlled, authoritative voice. "Dependents with no next of kin or legal guardian become wards of the state," he informs us. "Should your mother pass away, you will have little say in the matter."

No next of kin? What about Dad? I open my mouth to let him have it, but Cid beats me to it.

"We *have* a father," she shouts. "We never asked for your help and we don't want it!" She screams these last words and runs from the room.

Queenie and I exchange shocked looks. We don't need to say anything. Cid voiced all our concerns with more guts than either of us could have mustered. I have to hand it to her, too—old Charlie seems quite put out by the whole thing. He gathers his official documents, returning them to the briefcase as if they were the Dead Sea scrolls. He doesn't make eye contact with me again, he just claps the locks shut on his case and plucks it from the table. He hesitates for a moment, as though he is about to impart another bit of invaluable information, but apparently decides against it, and then he strides from the kitchen and down the stairs. As if on cue, the organ begins to groan, and for once I'm actually glad to hear it.

At the door, Charlie stops. He waits long enough to smooth his ruffled tail feathers before speaking over his shoulder. He says something like "I'll be in touch," but the impact of his exit is lost in the wails of the organ. The door sticks when he goes to open it, and he has to fumble with the lock before it yields. With as much dignity as he can summon, Charlie finally opens the door and disappears with a *bang*.

I rush down and lock the door behind him, then run back up, colliding with Queenie at the top of the stairs.

"Do you believe Cid's guts?" she says.

We tumble into Cid's room to congratulate the champ.

"That guy didn't know what hit him," I say, jumping like a wildman on Queenie's bed. "Cid's an animal!"

Queenie jumps next to me, whooping like a crazy chimp. "She's a hornet's nest! She's a swarm of bees!"

We shriek and howl in victory, and it's some time before we notice that Cid isn't joining in on the celebration. She's hunched soberly at the edge of her bed.

"What are we going to do?" she finally says.

"About the organ?" Queenie asks, still jumping from side to side.

"No. About everything. About Ma. You heard that creep. He was at the hospital, talking to the nurses. They think Ma is going to die."

Queenie drops as though shot. I thump to the floor in front of Cid.

"She's not going to die!" Queenie crumples to the bed and begins to wail.

"Look what you've done!" I turn to comfort Queenie. "It'll be okay," I tell her. "Ma won't die—she just can't."

But even as I say these words, my mind ricochets to that moment with the nurses in the hallway. *Hasn't got a snowball's chance in hell.* All of a sudden I'm furious again. How dare that nurse talk about Ma that way? How dare that rumpled little man come in here and tell us that we have no say in our own lives. What about Dad? He's next of kin, even if we don't know where he is. And I'm not going to just sit around and let someone decide what's best for us. The Duke would never allow it either. He'd go down, both guns blazing, cussing like a madman. These thoughts explode in my head until the pieces of my rage fall together at my feet and I stumble over an idea.

I'm going to find Dad and bring him home.

chapter 14

my quest begins

The girls have finally left the house to go visit Ma. It was all I could do to act normal while they puttered around getting ready. It took them nearly an hour just to eat a bowl of cereal. I think they would have been happy to sit around all day talking about what if's. What if Ma doesn't get better? What if the Children's Aid comes back? What if we never see one another again?

I haven't said a word about my plan to go get Dad. I think it's best if they don't know. They would just try to talk me out of it, or want to come along or something. I watch them walk across the park until they disappear from sight.

I go through my room, gathering the things I'm going to need for the road. I'm so hopped up on the idea of finding Dad that I can barely get organized. But I know that I have to move quickly or I'll lose my nerve. I think about the girl from the John Wayne movie, riding across the country to avenge her father's murder. She was only fourteen. What I'm trying to do is easier, I tell myself. I may not know where my father actually is, but at least I don't have to face a psychotic killer. I think Cid's right: Dad must be in Illinois, maybe even Brookfield, because that's where we used to live, and it would make sense for him to go back there.

I grab my sleeping bag, my compass, some socks and underwear, my second pair of jeans and some T-shirts. The clothes I stuff into my school knapsack. Then I excavate my old wineskin from a pile of stuff and sling it over my shoulder before emptying my cigar box of money. I have forty-eight dollars and sixty-three cents. If I'm going to make it at all, I'll have to be very frugal. I push the money into my pocket as I go into the kitchen to see what we have in the way of food.

There are a couple cans of maple baked beans that I take. I choose a box of cinnamon Pop-Tarts but pass on the KD, because I won't be bringing milk or margarine. They'll just go bad. I haven't much room in the saddle-bags, so I'll have to pack carefully to make everything fit. I grab a small bag of cornmeal, thinking I can make corn dodgers like the ones The Duke ate in the movie. All you need is water and some fat of some kind, I think. I take a brick of shortening, a couple cans of tuna and some tins of sardines. I hesitate over the jellies, then choose a small jar of grape, my favourite. The sugar will help keep my spirits up. I'll buy some chocolate bars and gum along the way too. A small saucepan from the cupboard will suffice for cooking. It's an old one that no one will miss, with a scratched copper bottom and a dented lid. It will do for boiling water and heating up beans and things. I take some matches and a set of old silver-plated cutlery, then rinse the wineskin. It has a funny, vinyl smell that doesn't want to come out but I fill it with water and cap it all the same. I have to make sure I don't let myself get dehydrated in the summer heat.

When I'm done scavenging in the kitchen, I put the food in bags and haul my kit to the top of the stairs. Once there, I realize I've forgotten a can opener for the tinned items and go back into the kitchen. We haven't but one, an old hand-cranker, so Cid and Queenie will have to either borrow one or buy another. I leave a dollar for that purpose on the kitchen table and scribble a note:

gone to find Dad—
I took the can opener

I don't sign my name. I figure Cid and Queenie will know who the note is from. I guess I don't want anyone else coming across the note and trying to stop me. There's so much more that I want to say to the girls but I don't even know where to start. I hope that they will be okay, and that the Children's Aid will stay away until I get back. I hope that Ma is miraculously better and all of this will just be a distant memory some day, a story that we can choose to remember or forget. The dollar bill and note look so forlorn on the table, it makes my heart ache. Will Queenie and Cid be all right? What if something awful happens while I'm away? What if Ma dies . . .? I can feel my resolve start to sputter. I replace the dollar bill with a five, stash the can opener in one of the bags, then hurry down the stairs before I change my mind.

When I get to the door, I stop again. Dad might not recognize me after all these years. I was just a child when he left. I've changed so much since then. And how will I recognize him? Do I even remember what he looks like? How will I convince him that I'm his son?

It comes to me like a thunderbolt. The uniform. I'll bring Dad's picture and his uniform, proof of who I am and that I know him too. I race back upstairs and rummage for the uniform under my bed. I take Dad's picture from the drawer in my night table and slip the one of me in the silver Pontiac into my back pocket. I look around my room for just a moment, then trot down the stairs and out the door with my things.

It isn't easy walking to the barn with all these bags of stuff. Twice I have to rest, switching the load around to give my hands a break. By the time I reach the stable, my arms are aching and I'm sweating like a horse. I'm tired and not very sure of myself. But then an image of the rumpled man jumps into my mind and my determination grows stronger than before. I bustle into the barn and run right into the pack of snotty girls.

They stop talking immediately. Alyson is standing among them and I can feel her eyes on me. I shift the plastic bags in my hands. One of the girls snorts disdainfully. I feel like a beggar or a homeless person. I wish I didn't have to walk past them, but there's no other way to get to Smokey's stall. Eyes focused on some point at the end of the aisle, I steel myself and walk on, the stupid bags rustling loudly as they twist and bang against my legs.

"Running away from home?" one of the girls says as I rustle past. The others laugh. But not Alyson. She looks away, eyes lowered.

When I reach Smokey's stall, he nickers excitedly. I didn't think to bring him a treat, I was in such a hurry. I hope he isn't disappointed. The cans clatter noisily as I drop the bags in a heap beside the stall and open the door. Smokey shuffles up to me, nosing my pockets, expecting to find a piece of carrot or apple.

"I'm sorry, buddy," I say. "I'll give you something later . . . I promise."

He munches serenely on whatever bit of hay he has in his mouth, completely unaware of the adventure we're about to take. I put his halter on and lead him to the cross-ties. I brush him good and long because I know that this is going to be a hard ride for us both. I take extra care picking his hooves and checking to see that his feet are all right. His hooves could use a bit of a trim but other than that, they're fine. There are a pair of nippers hanging on a nail at the other end of the barn but I'm not about to cross paths with those girls again so I leave well enough alone.

When I'm done grooming Smokey, I slowly start to saddle him. I tighten the cinch and make sure that the blanket Mr. Thompson gave us is smooth and unwrinkled. I don't want Smokey to get sore. I adjust the stirrups and tie the saddlebags to the back of the saddle. Smokey watches warily as I start to load them up. He must wonder what's going on. I'm sure he's suspicious of the extra weight. I pack carefully to distribute the supplies properly and maximize space. There's just enough room for everything, including the hoof pick and a brush, and I'm pleased that the bags hold much more than I had thought.

I fiddle with this and that, adjusting straps and retightening the cinch, waiting for the group of girls to leave so I can go without being harassed. I check Dad's watch. It's nearly twelve o'clock already. The nurse will be in Ma's room, changing her IV and administering some medicine or other. Cid and Queenie will be there, thinking about the morning and what will happen with the rumpled man. They have no idea that there is a note waiting for them when they get home and that I'll be gone.

The girls finally leave the barn, snickering over something—at the expense of someone else, no doubt. Taking the opportunity to make a quick exit, I unhook Smokey from the cross-ties and bridle him. I cluck with my tongue, urging him past the other stalls to the door. My mind is a pinwheel, spinning with thoughts of what lies ahead. Smokey's hooves click softly against the concrete floor. We navigate the corner, only to bump head-on into Alyson. She looks at me, her face serious and beautiful and concerned.

"*Are* you running away?" she asks.

I try to hide my surprise but it doesn't work. Her gaze feels like hot coals against my skin. I stammer, betraying my nervousness. "I—I'm not running away . . . I'm looking for someone." I shift my feet, working the reins into a ball in my hands.

"Where are you going?" she asks me. "You can't just leave."

For an instant, everything changes. I'm so flattered by her attention that for a moment I actually believe that she likes me. Not as a friend. As a boy. Suddenly, I want to tell her everything. I want to explain about Ma and the rumpled man and what Cid said. I want to tell her that I'm going on a journey to find my father and that I have all the things I need to get me there. I'll sleep out under the stars, I won't be afraid, and I will come back, she needn't worry. But then I catch a look in her eyes and discover that I'm way off the mark. She's at least three years older than me. I'm just a kid to her. She isn't asking me to stay because she likes me. She's just concerned in the way a big sister is for her younger siblings. She even feels sorry for me.

She says, "Does your mother know where you're going? What about Queenie and Cid?"

"Don't worry about me," I say. I cluck Smokey forward and leave Alyson standing in the aisle.

Guiding Smokey through the door into the parking lot, I mount quickly, so he won't have a chance to complain about the extra weight of the saddlebags. He pins his ears back as I squeeze my heels into his sides, but he doesn't buck. I don't hesitate for a second, not even to take one last look around, because I imagine that Alyson is watching me from one of the barn windows, and I don't want to lose my resolve. I would like to see Ma once more before I leave but know that I can't.

Pushing the idea from my mind, I think about the direction I'm heading. I think about where I may end up, and how I'll get there. I'll take the road to the woods, then follow my compass southwest, toward Illinois. Like I said before, I have no idea if Dad is even there, but it's a good starting point. If I cross the border south of Sarnia, where the population is small, I'm less likely to get caught. I'll skirt towns and avoid people as much as possible, sticking to the back roads. I'll keep going, until I find Dad or die trying. But first I have to go to the meadow to get Lazy Boy.

* * *

Smokey moves at a good pace, picking up his feet and looking around at the cars as they speed by. He doesn't shy at the vehicles, he watches inquisitively as they zoom past. Some people slow down to take a look at us and the whole adventure has an air of festivity. I have to admit, it feels good to be riding Smokey in the afternoon sun. I have Glen Campbell's "Rhinestone Cowboy" looping through my head. Smokey seems to move to the beat of the song as we swing along on the shoulder of the road. For a while I even forget what I'm setting out to do. I feel like a *coureur de bois,* a French trapper, making my way into the Canadian wilderness. I've always wanted to live like a *coureur de bois,* hunting and building shelters and trading for things. I wish I'd brought a hat, though. My head feels like a boiled egg already from the sun. My lips are dry too. The air is dusty and hot from the heat and the cars.

At last we turn off the road to the park. Smokey lopes to the woods that lead to the meadow. The forest is cool and dark after the heat off the road. Smokey groans and slows to a walk. I pat him on the neck and let him set the pace. He pricks up his ears, listening. Sparrows twitter. Red squirrels scold each other in the trees. There's so much to see with all the plants and animals that it doesn't seem long before we reach the clearing where the woods give way to a rolling sea of summer grass. It's so tall it swishes past my feet in the stirrups. Bugs click and spring out of the way as we move toward the old cedar that holds Lazy Boy. It stands out against the backdrop of forest like a shimmering ghost.

I pull Smokey up to the trunk and peer inside. I can't see Lazy Boy and for one horrible second I think that maybe somebody stole it. Reaching my hand into the opening, I feel frantically around, stretching my fingers as far as they'll go. I stand up in the stirrups, which Smokey doesn't like, until my hand finally brushes against the butt of the rifle.

"Whoa, Smokey," I say, trying to steady him as I pull the rifle from the tree. I clean the dust and the cobwebs off with my shirt. Lazy Boy looks as great as I remember. I don't have any bullets, so the rifle is pretty much useless for self-defence, unless I decide to throw it at somebody. Still, I feel better just knowing that I have it with me. I push it through one of the leather loops at the front of the saddle and cover it with my kangaroo jacket. My stomach rumbles. I'm hungry already. But I'll have to wait until I've made some headway and can set up camp before I'll allow myself to eat. It's two-thirty and I want to cover some ground before nightfall. Thankfully it's summer. It will stay light until nine o'clock.

Smokey grows impatient with all the standing around. He tosses his head and chomps on the bit. He stamps his foot, urging me to get on with things. I pull out my compass. The little arrow sways and jiggles then holds as I rein Smokey southwest, into the sun.

* * *

We ride for hours, over country roads and through fields, crossing small creeks with cattle standing knee-deep in black muck. They gaze at us with curiosity, water and grass dripping from their droopy mouths. Farms dot the countryside. Fields of wheat and hay gleam beneath a cloudless sky. The sun follows our journey, tracing a slow arc above the trees on the horizon. An occasional car drives by, but for the most part we are on our own. It isn't difficult to escape people in these parts once you leave the city.

Over the hours, my pride in Smokey continues to grow. He doesn't question the purpose of our journey. He navigates the terrain with confidence and interest. I give him his head crossing streams so he can step safely over stones and through the slippery mud. In fact, I pretty much put Smokey on autopilot and enjoy the view, taking regular sips from the wineskin to keep my fluids up, as Ma would say. The water is warm and tastes of plastic, but it's better than nothing.

When we enter the woods, a couple of deerflies show up, orbiting my head like annoying little satellites. I swat at them but they come right back, buzzing and whirling around. They won't land because we're moving, so I try to forget about them by letting my mind wander. I think about Ma and the girls. I wonder if they've found my note yet. Will they call the police, the way Ma did last time I was missing? I hope they aren't too worried about me. I envision my first meeting with Dad, playing the scene out like a movie in my mind. I imagine his surprise and all the things we'll say. I'm bold, like The Duke, but kind and forgiving too. Dad's sorry and overjoyed to see me. Between all these thoughts, Alyson floats in and out. She's beautiful and loving, admiring my courage and strength.

By dusk, the deerflies have disappeared and the mosquitoes have taken their place. My back and feet are aching and my stomach is roaring for food. It's time to make camp. I manage to find a sheltered spot next to a pond with a trickling stream. Pulling Lazy Boy from the saddle, I dismount, placing the rifle on a tree stump. Smokey is happy to be free of the bit. I attach the lead to his halter and tie him to a branch. The saddlebags feel heavier now than when we started because I'm hungry and sore and tired. I hang them up in a tree, then loosen Smokey's cinch and remove the saddle. Smokey snorts and groans with gratitude. He closes his eyes and lowers his head as I brush him. I give him a long rub-down to soothe his muscles. He has to be good and cool before I let him drink so that he doesn't get sick. He stretches his neck and closes his eyes as I scrub his face and behind his ears. Once I've picked his hooves and checked him all over, I lead him to the river. He makes loud slurping noises as he guzzles the water, stepping into the stream so that the water rushes over his feet.

When he's had his fill, I tether Smokey so he can graze, then scarf a package of Pop-Tarts to tide me over. I finish them both in two or three bites, I'm so hungry.

The fire is next. I start gathering wood, collecting small, dry twigs and birchbark for kindling. The bigger branches I break into more manageable pieces. I even find a couple of thick, dry logs that will burn for hours once the fire has a good bed of coals. I stack all of it into a big pile, commending myself for the skill I acquired over the years building fires at our old house. I'm pretty much a master when it comes to burning wood. When I have enough fuel to last the night, I build a firepit with a bunch of rocks, placing them in a circle on a bare patch of ground.

The twigs and birchbark leap to life, burning hot and fast. The flames lap greedily as I feed more and bigger sticks into the fire. Its orange tongues flicker at the setting sun, a melting scoop of pink sherbet in the darkening sky. The temperature begins to drop and the mosquitoes wage a full-scale attack. I dig through my knapsack for my sweatshirt and find a book. It's a skinny volume of poems by Robert Frost that I never returned to the library. I must owe a thousand dollars on this book, I've had it for so long. I stuff it back in my knapsack and decide to wear my kangaroo jacket, zipping it up to my chin and tying the hood tight around my face. From the saddlebags, I produce a can of beans, the set of cutlery and the can opener. The opener catches the firelight as it bites into the can of beans, and I'm struck by the loneliness of being out here by myself. It's a lot harder to be cheerful now that the sun is going down. I wonder if The Duke ever feels this way.

The beans are going to taste good, though. Prying open the can, I scoop the contents into my little pot, scraping every last bean from the bottom of the tin. I place the pot on one of the campfire stones and let the flames work their magic. The mosquitoes are unbearable, so I unroll my sleeping bag and sit on it, leaning close to the fire to discourage the bugs from biting my face. Their high-pitched whines fill my ears.

As the beans simmer, I watch the sun dissolve into a scarlet puddle over the trees. From deep within the woods, an owl hoots mournfully. Smokey raises his head, listening, his eyes glowing and wide in the firelight. I try to ignore the pesky mosquitoes and focus on the delicious beans that I'm about to eat. The smell of maple and woodsmoke drifts invitingly in the air. I tilt my head back, resting against a rock. The constellations twinkle above me. They seem to shift and vibrate in the ocean of sky, uncertain at first, then growing more confident as the last of the sun's light flashes like a fish scale and slips quietly away. There is no moon, so the stars shine all the brighter, until several seem to fall and blink right in front of me. Fireflies! They dip and bob along, their little lanterns like beacons in the dark.

I nudge the pot of beans with my foot, turning it slightly to distribute the heat. I think about Ma and Queenie and Cid, and pray that they're all right. A wave of sadness rises inside me. I'm out here. In the woods. By myself.

"By myself," I say aloud.

From somewhere beyond the circle of light, a twig snaps. Smokey steps to one side, his eyes searching. I stretch my foot out to turn the pot again when another twig snaps—this time it's closer and louder. Bolting upright, I practically kick the beans into the fire. My heart thrums in my ears as I strain to listen. It's probably just a deer, I tell myself. Or a raccoon. Or some innocent red squirrel up way past its bedtime.

I look around for Lazy Boy, just in case, then curse myself when I remember that I've left the rifle on the tree stump. I'll have to leave the safety of the fire to get it. The flames tug at the hem of darkness around me. Why did I leave the rifle just sitting out there? The Duke would never have done anything so dumb. Thoughts of Charlie Chaplin's coffin dance in my head. Picking up my knife and fork, I hold the cutlery in my fists like a deranged customer at an all-night diner. Smokey rumbles cautiously, then gives a short, high whinny. There is a strange rustling sound behind me. I have to get the rifle. Gathering my courage, I take a step forward.

But the beans! I can't let them burn. I reach for the pot handle and snatch my hand back from the heat. The metal is burning hot from the fire. Using the sleeve of my jacket for protection, I quickly pluck the pot from the stone, placing it on the ground. I hold the knife and fork out in front of me again and step from the light. I can't see a thing. My eyes are blind from staring into the fire. I scan the area, searching for Lazy Boy. There is a loud clatter behind me and Smokey squeals in fear. He stamps around, trying to pull himself free. I lunge forward, dropping the knife and fork to the ground as I find the rifle, snatch it up and cock the lever.

"I've got a gun!" I shout.

With shaking hands, I hold Lazy Boy against my shoulder as though to shoot. There's a scuffling sound and I cock the gun again to let whoever it is know that I'm not kidding. I stand, rifle poised, too terrified to move. The fire starts to wane and I'm worried that it will go out. My eyes finally adjust to the light and I can see Smokey, a pale shape in the night, still tied to the tree branch despite his efforts to get free. As the minutes tick by and nothing happens, I begin to feel bolder. Rifle still held to my shoulder, I walk slowly toward the fire. When I reach the firepit, I see that I've been robbed.

The pot of beans is missing. Only the lid is left, discarded on the ground. Fear and anger clash in my chest and I'm not sure whether to be afraid of the thief or enraged that my dinner is gone. What's worse, my cutlery is somewhere out in the woods and the rest of the food is in the saddlebags. At least they didn't try to hurt me or Smokey. I should be glad for that, I guess. But they stole my beans and I haven't got the guts to get something else to eat from the saddlebags. They're up in the tree, and the thief could still be lurking around out there in the dark.

The fire sputters. I feed it with twigs until it dances again. I put one of the big logs on and tend it carefully so it will burn slowly and long. Then I inch over to Smokey and untie him, bringing him over to the fire. I hold his lead in my hand just in case I have to make a quick getaway. Stomach growling, I stare into the flames, Lazy Boy across my lap, my eyes growing heavier and heavier with each minute that crawls past. But whenever I'm about to sleep, my head snaps up and I force myself awake. I don't want to be caught off guard again. I'm terrified and homesick already and decide at that moment that I will turn around and go home as soon as it's light—no matter what The Duke would do.

chapter 15

dogged by the devil

I'm tickled awake by something nibbling at my cheek. It's Smokey, mouthing my face to get my attention. Where am I? I shake my head to get the fluff out then check Dad's watch: 7:30 a.m. I made it through the night! I even managed to sleep. Lazy Boy is still lying across my lap. The campfire is now just a pile of grey ash. Flies buzz drowsily in the morning light. Smokey swishes his tail to chase them away. He lowers his head and blows softly against my face to say good morning. I stroke his muzzle, grateful that he stayed beside me all night. He didn't even try to wander off.

"You're such a good boy," I tell him.

My body aches and cracks like old wood as I stand up. My face feels burned, from the sun or the campfire or the mosquitoes, I can't tell which. I'm just happy that both of us are all right. Looking around, I can see that everything is exactly as I left it. The saddle is still on its end, blanket draped overtop. The saddlebags are unmolested in the tree; my knapsack leans to one side. The knife and fork lie where I dropped them at the base of the old tree stump. It seems silly to have been so scared in the night, now that the sun is up. It dances through the leaves, winking brightly, and flashes off the stolen saucepan lying in the grass just a few yards from where I slept. The thief ate the beans right under my nose! I feel sick at the thought of someone standing in the dark, so close, yet undetected. But the sunlight smiles back at me, chasing my fears away, and I decide that I can go on with my journey after all.

I pick up the pan and look inside. Whoever ate the beans sure was hungry. They practically scrubbed the pot clean. I have to wonder if I would have done the same in different circumstances. I suppose anyone could do such a thing if they were starving and desperate. Still, I hope whoever stole my food is long gone by now.

I lead Smokey to the river. He sniffs and nibbles at the water, making small ripples in the surface before settling in to drink. I dip the saucepan in the river and wash it clean. Then I cup water in my hands and splash my face. Smokey seems amused by this. He watches me, his mouth drooling water, his lower lip slack and comical.

"Haven't you ever seen someone wash their face before?" I say. I splash a little water at him in fun. His bottom lip quivers as though he's laughing, and I have to laugh back. Sometimes I think he's smarter than a person, the way he looks at me.

Running my tongue across my teeth, I realize with dismay that I've forgotten my toothbrush. I'll have to buy one the first chance I get. For now, I take a twig and splinter one end so that it looks like a small broom. I dip it into the water and work the stick across my teeth until they squeak. Smokey continues to watch me. "You want to try?" I hold the stick out to him. He sniffs, testing the smell, before nibbling delicately, then he snorts and shakes his head. I toss the stick to the ground and give myself a good stretch.

Smokey plods along behind me like a big dog, dragging his lead as I set about breaking camp. I douse the ashes with water then scatter the fire stones to hide my tracks. The remaining firewood I toss randomly about. The knife and fork I rinse in the river. Then I organize the saddlebags and my knapsack. My stomach grumbles loudly, reminding me that I've only had a couple of Pop-Tarts since breakfast yesterday. Opening a can of tuna, I stuff the meat into my mouth with my fingers, the juice running down my chin. When the can is empty, I actually drink the rest of the juice, because it smells and tastes pretty good at this point. But what to do with the empty cans? Burying them in the woods would be disrespectful. Instead I rinse them in the river then flatten them with my foot, pushing the lids inside when I'm done to avoid cutting myself later on. They don't take up much room in the saddlebags now that they're flattened. I'll throw them out the first chance I get.

I fill the wineskin with water from the river, then brush and saddle Smokey, securing the saddlebags. After putting on my knapsack, I grab Lazy Boy and mount, slipping the rifle into the leather loop beside my leg. A quick check of the compass is all I need and we're off on the second day of our journey.

We cross the river at a shallow spot, the sunlight glinting off the pebbles under the water. The day looks promising: calm and clear and not too hot. The deer-flies are nowhere in sight. Birds serenade us as we move through the woods. For miles and miles before us, the forest stretches seamlessly. This makes it difficult to gauge our direction so I check my compass often to make sure we haven't ridden off course. Smokey is moving at a steady, comfortable pace. I relax, keeping the reins slack. The saddle feels good, despite how sore I am from riding and sleeping on the ground. It squeaks and creaks with newness, which I find comforting. I think about Ma and Queenie and Cid and wonder what they are doing. I try to fill my head with good ideas, and mostly I'm successful, except I can't shake the feeling that someone is following me.

I look left and right, not too obviously, hoping to catch a glimpse of whoever it may be. The forest is a patchwork of shadow and light. There are lots of places for a person to hide. I hum to myself as a distraction. A crow squawks over my head. Reining Smokey to a stop, I twist quickly around in the saddle. The poplars shake their leaves. It sounds like water rushing. I squint my eyes, scanning the forest. Something seems to move in the shadows that fill our wake. But it's just the sun, dipping in and out of the trees. The crow squawks again, telling us to move along. I give Smokey a nudge and he starts to walk. He cocks his ears back and forth, listening. Gripping the horn with one hand, I gather the reins with the other as a precaution.

After an hour or so of vigilance, nothing out of the ordinary happens. I let down my guard and practise spinning the rifle like The Duke. It's a bit awkward at first, but after a few spins I get the hang of it again. For several hours I spin the gun, over and over, until I can do it effortlessly. It reminds me of Queenie and Cid in the meadow and my spirits flag a little. I miss them so much. But I push my sadness aside with happier thoughts to keep myself together.

By noon, I'm starving and Smokey could use a break. We stop beside a small creek trickling through the woods. I grab another pack of Pop-Tarts from the saddlebags, holding the foil package in my teeth as I loosen the cinch on Smokey's saddle. I leave the saddle on, but remove the bridle and let it hang over Smokey's neck so he can graze. Still clenching the Pop-Tarts in my teeth, I relieve myself behind a tree then find a nice big rock to sit on, tossing my knapsack on the ground at my feet.

The Pop-Tarts smell like cinnamon heaven when I open the pack. My mouth waters as I breathe in deeply. I want to eat both at once, wolfing them down in two or three bites the way I did before, but I don't. I only eat one, very slowly, savouring it like it's the most expensive pastry ever made, because I have no idea how long it's going to be before I can buy more. My stomach groans as I zip the remaining Pop-Tart into my knapsack for later. Sitting on the rock, I torture myself with thoughts of my favourite meal: lasagna, with fresh dinner rolls, hot from the oven, string beans and lots of Parmesan cheese. Smokey forages for greens, while I daydream about food. He's probably feeling the same, wishing for a sweet piece of apple or carrot to take the edge off. As though reading my mind, he plods over to where I'm sitting and nuzzles my shirt pocket.

"Time to go, buddy," I say, scrubbing his forelock. "We'll buy some apples the first chance we get, I promise."

Smokey stands obediently as I tighten the cinch. He doesn't puff up any more the way he did when I first put the saddle on him. But he's staring nervously over my shoulder at something. As I lower the stirrup, I have the overwhelming feeling that we're being watched. Instantly, my skin turns to gooseflesh and the tiny hairs stand up on the back of my neck. I'm too terrified to turn around and look. I finish adjusting the saddle with as little movement as possible, then slip Smokey's bridle on, my hands shaking like the poplar leaves. Crazy images invade my thoughts— of me, fighting for my life, and Smokey bolting riderless through the woods, the stirrups slapping angrily against his ribs. I see Cid and Queenie crying, and Ma in her hospital bed. Then Charlie Chaplin's coffin pops up, his shrivelled body inside.

At last the bridle is secure and I spring into the saddle. But I've forgotten my knapsack on the ground! I hesitate for a second, wondering what to do. I need my clothes. And Dad's uniform, and my Pop-Tarts are in the knapsack too. Taking a quick breath, I jump down, snatch up the bag and mount again, all in one motion. I don't wait to find my seat, I just whip Smokey straight into a canter, the knapsack looped over my arm, my feet fumbling for the stirrups as we run. From the corner of my eye, I see something dart out from behind a bush to my right. I can't tell what it is, but it's black as Hades and flashing with teeth. Smokey senses my fear, breaking into a gallop, his mane flying, his hooves pounding against the ground. I lean forward and give him his head, yelling:

"Get up, Smokey! Come on!"

We thunder through the woods, the knapsack bouncing wildly on my arm, the trees snatching at my hair and legs. A low branch appears and nearly knocks me from the saddle but I duck just in time, barely making it under. The scenery is a crazy blur until another branch appears in front of us, huge and dark. For one second everything seems to freeze as I duck. The branch misses me by inches but snags the knapsack and tears it from my arm, nearly wrenching my shoulder from its socket. The bag hits the ground, bouncing and tumbling like a football for several feet. I'm about to stop and get it when I see the beast, charging up behind us. It's a dog, as big as a wolf, with fur as black as midnight. It rushes up and starts tearing at the knapsack.

I rein Smokey around and turn to face the animal. It's matted and filthy and has the haunted look of starvation. Smokey tosses his head, stepping backwards and sideways, his ribs heaving from the gallop. He chomps on the bit, too frightened to stand still. To my horror, the creature grabs one of the straps on the knapsack and begins dragging it back into the woods. I start hollering at the top of my lungs:

"Hey! Get away from there! Go on!"

The dog stops and looks at me, strap still clenched between its teeth. I pull Lazy Boy from the saddle and wave it like a madman over my head.

"Get out of here, you filthy mongrel!"

The sight of the rifle sends the dog into a frenzy. It snarls and snaps as though to lunge. I make to throw the rifle like a javelin. The dog goes wild. Obviously it's had some bad experience with a rifle before. I break off a tree branch and throw it. The dog shies, just enough to give me courage. I kick Smokey forward, throwing branches and yelling for the dog to get lost.

This seems to work. The mutt drops the bag and dashes into the woods, hiding behind a maple tree. Leaning over, I keep my eye on the dog as I use Lazy Boy to spear the bag, slinging it up onto the saddle. The dog watches me with hungry eyes as I put on the knapsack, adjusting the straps so that it's snug. Once the bag is secure, I give a savage shout, just to let the mongrel know I mean business, then canter off.

I look back to see the dog following us about thirty feet behind. I rein Smokey around. The dog stops dead in its tracks, staring. I shout and it cringes, but it doesn't run away. Smokey and I take off again, this time at a trot. The dog follows, keeping its distance. I slow Smokey to a walk and the dog slows too. We trot and it trots, pink tongue lolling from its mouth, head slightly lowered. It paces us like this for miles, always staying far enough away to avoid me.

We reach a small clearing in the woods next to a pond. It's nearly dusk so I decide to stop for the night and make camp. Smokey is grateful for the grass that grows in big tufts all around the water. I unsaddle him and brush him, keeping the gear close at hand. The whole time, the dog skulks along the thirty-foot perimeter of our camp, watching and waiting. Clipping the lead to Smokey's halter, I tether him loosely to a branch, then begin to look for stones and wood to build a campfire. I carry Lazy Boy with me everywhere, gathering a few more stones than necessary—good baseball-sized ones that I can throw if need be. I stack them in a pile next to the fire, beside the saddle and my knapsack. The dog lies down, panting.

While I build the fire and prepare to make corn dodgers, I keep one eye on the dog, my gear practically under my feet. I have no idea how to make the dodgers, but I want something toothsome so badly I could scream. I mix the dough in the saucepan, working the cornmeal with the water and shortening. Once it's good and blended, I scrape the dough into a ball and knead it with my hands. Adding another chunk of shortening to the pan, I place it by the fire to heat. The shortening begins to sizzle. I start tossing pieces of dough into the pan, flattening them into cakes with the fork and frying them until they're brown. They smell great and I can hardly wait until they're cooked to start eating. The dog watches, licking its lips as I slather grape jelly onto the cakes. The first one burns my tongue, I swallow it down so quickly. I eat four or five like this, until the hole in my stomach begins to fill. When I finally slow down enough to actually taste the cakes, I can tell that they're hard and a bit bland for the lack of salt. But the jelly makes up for the fact that they aren't very good. They satisfy my hunger, and I only wish that I had a nice cup of coffee to wash them down.

I eat all but three of the dodgers. Those go in my jacket pocket for later. I've managed to forget about the dog, and when I finally look up from my feed, I see that it has inched its way closer to my camp. I pick up a rock and stand with my fist in the air.

"Get lost!"

Smokey looks up, startled by my shouting. The dog slinks slowly back and lowers itself to the ground. It watches me menacingly. I keep the rock close at hand as I tend to my needs. I've forgotten toilet paper so I have to use leaves. When I'm finished, I watch Smokey grazing until the sun has almost slipped below the trees and the fireflies and mosquitoes reappear. To protect my face from bites, I take a glob of mud from the pond and smear it over my skin. It smells funny, but if it keeps the mosquitoes away, I don't care.

I look over at the mutt again. I don't trust it one bit, so I lead Smokey close to the fire and tether him next to me. The fire crackles warmly. Banking the coals, I add another log. Smokey noses me softly as I climb into my sleeping bag and nestle in. The dog's eyes shimmer in the dark. It's out there, hungry and vicious, a desperate criminal waiting to catch us off guard. I understand now that it was the dog that stole my beans, licking the saucepan clean. But where did it come from and how did it manage to survive this long? Is it a stray? A castoff? A runaway?

Because I'm not ready to sleep, I pull Robert Frost's poems from my knapsack and read for a bit. The first poem is called "Out, Out—" and it does little to ease my mind. It's about a boy who cuts off his own hand with a chainsaw and dies. It sends a shiver up my spine. I read the next, "The Death of the Hired Man," about a poor man who dies in someone else's house, because it's the only home he knows, I guess. The poems are dark and sad and I have to wonder: are all poets this depressing? I read one more. "Stopping by Woods on a Snowy Evening." I like it best of all, although it's about death too. But it has a horse in it and I like the way it rhymes. The last part stays with me, the words rolling over and over in my mind. *But I have promises to keep, and miles to go before I sleep. And miles to go before I sleep.* I close the book, feeling just like the man from the poem, even though I'm bedded down for the night. We both have promises to keep and miles to go before we sleep, so to speak.

I tuck Mr. Frost back into my knapsack. His poetry has made me thoughtful, and I'm reminded of a dog we once had but never loved. His name was Rusty. Dad took him from a man and his son as payment for a debt owed. The boy's face was innocent and unknowing as he carried the dog's dish into our backyard, the mutt trotting faithfully beside him. I remember how the father shook Dad's hand, and the way he ushered his son away afterwards, the boy's face now crumpled with confusion. He didn't understand why he had to give his dog away. To us, the mutt was feral and strangely detached. It broke its chain repeatedly, searching for the boy. It wasn't more than a week before it was hit by a truck on the highway and killed. We buried him in the backyard beneath a pine tree, each shovelful of dirt an accusation against Dad for taking something he had no right to.

My mind turns to the wild dog, waiting in the darkness. Maybe it's a dog like Rusty, abandoned and unloved.

I feel a twinge of sympathy for it. Still, I have to admit that I'm afraid. Afraid the dog has rabies or bad intentions and will try to attack sometime in the night. If it is part wolf—which it seems to be—it would be stupid to trust it, I tell myself. After all, there's no denying it would have taken my knapsack and ripped it to pieces over a Pop-Tart. And then where would I be? I think of the food in the saddlebags. I lean over and grab the bags, shoving them under my head for safekeeping. The mud from the pond has started to dry and crack off my skin, and it's making my face feel all tight. I get the idea to mix it with shortening the next time so it will stay moist. Lazy Boy across my lap, I stare at the sky, trying to stay awake by guessing at constellations. But it isn't long before I fall sleep.

In the middle of the night I'm jolted awake. Something's pulling on my arm! I bolt upright, Lazy Boy at the ready. It's Smokey, tugging on the lead. He shifts anxiously beside me. Wrestling a half-burned log from the fire, I hold it up so that I can see. The fire catches the dog's eyes and sets them glowing. It's no more than ten feet from the camp. I wave the flaming log savagely, yelling at the dog to get back. It ignores me, emboldened by the dark. Sparks explode on the ground as I throw the log at the mutt, sending it skulking into the woods. I set a few more branches on the fire for good measure. The log shimmers on the ground where it landed. I watch to be sure it doesn't set anything on fire as I slowly sink off to sleep again.

In the morning all is clear. The dog is nowhere to be seen. I tether Smokey in the grassy clearing then go about my morning chores. I check the log that I threw to be sure it's good and out. Tossing it onto the camp-fire, I douse the lot with water from the pond. I eat the leftover Pop-Tart from my knapsack and decide to keep all food in the saddlebags from now on. I've forgotten about the mud on my face until I catch my reflection in the pond. I look insane, but the mud actually helped to keep the mosquitoes at bay so I don't care. The water isn't as clear and fresh as that in the little river I bathed in yesterday, but I do my best to wash up. Once my face is clean, I brush my teeth using a twig the way I did before. When everything is taken care of, I saddle Smokey and gear up.

I'm just about to mount when I see the dog, crawl-ing out from behind a tree. It creeps forward, belly touching the ground, head lowered submissively. I think it must be hurt or rabid or trying to trick me, but then it stops and looks up hopefully. Smokey steps ner-vously as I mount. I place my hand on Lazy Boy. The dog crawls forward another foot and stops again, the same forlorn look on its face. It's so pitiful, so cowed, that I actually feel sorry for it. The memory of Rusty tugs at my conscience. Reaching into my pocket, I do something that I know I will probably regret. I toss the mutt a corn dodger. It lunges at the dodger, gobbling it up in a feverish gulp. Then it stands and looks at me for more, smacking its lips expectantly.

I rein Smokey around and start the day's journey. The dog follows behind, keeping its distance, but keeping up. We're a strange caravan: me on Smokey, and the dog trotting tirelessly behind us.

Eventually, the forest opens to a huge meadow. The land is lonely and dry. The wind talks through the grasses. Scrubby trees stand here and there. Prickly hawthorns and sour crabs, with a few scabby McIntoshes, too, long since abandoned and left to grow untended. I pick a few for Smokey and nibble at a couple myself. They're a little sour, but it's nice to taste something fresh.

Now that we've left the woods, the sun beats mercilessly down on us. I tie a T-shirt around my head for protection, dampening it with some water from the wineskin to keep me cool. I smear some shortening on my lips. They're as dry and cracked as the land. I wish I had some Chapstick. I feel sorry for the dog with all that black fur.

After a while, we come upon a wooden shack, broken down and leaning to one side on a small hill. Some homesteader's attempt at eking out an existence in the Canadian wilderness. We linger to inspect it, the dog panting about twenty feet back. There's nothing inside the shack but a bunch of old newspapers, the skeleton of a bicycle (no wheels) and an old porcelain sink. Smokey shakes his head, swishing away the flies that gather the moment we stop. We continue on our way, me checking the compass at regular intervals. After an hour or so, we cross a gravel road that cuts straight across the meadow. Fences start to appear and a few farms speckle the horizon. I wish I knew where we were. We'll have to be careful not to get caught trespassing.

We follow a fencerow for several miles as it dips and stretches across the grassland. Cattle graze peacefully in the fields. They watch as we move past. After another hour or two, we reach the woods again. There's a river that bubbles and dances just inside the forest edge. It's a good place to stop for a rest and something to eat. We all take a long, deep drink of water from the river, including the dog. He keeps his distance, taking up a position on the periphery of the camp, panting beneath the shade of a mulberry bush. I make a note to pick some berries before we leave.

I'm hungry and a bit dizzy from the sun, but I'm getting better at setting up camp and I have a fire going in no time. I heat up the last of the maple beans to eat with the remaining corn dodgers. The sweet smell filters into the air. I'm just about to take the pot from the fire when I see something that makes me jump.

It's a man, standing on the edge of the woods, watching me.

chapter 16
greed

I face the man, rifle in hand. He's like a stock character from a movie. All arms and legs, with a stubbly beard. He's filthy and his clothes hang like bags from his body. His shoes are worn and coming apart at the soles. A piece of binder twine holds up his pants. His face is shielded in part by a floppy kind of hat, but I can still see his eyes. They're small and dark and beady, shifting back and forth, from me to the beans to Smokey to the saddle. I don't know where he came from but I can see that he's up to no good. He takes a step forward, working his jaw as though to speak.

"Them beans you're cooking?"

I tighten my grip on Lazy Boy.

"I can always tell the smell of beans . . . and those smell mighty good." He takes another step, nodding at the saddle. "That's some fine rig you got there. Must have cost a pretty penny."

I keep my eyes on him. I don't dare look away.

He assumes a posture of friendliness, his hands outstretched at his sides. "Come on, son. Can't you share a little sup with a hungry man?" He moves a couple of steps closer.

"That's far enough, mister," I finally say, gesturing with Lazy Boy.

He puts his hands in the air, smiling, his teeth two rows of rotten corn. He steps again. "I don't want no trouble."

Raising Lazy Boy to my shoulder, I sight the man, my heart thumping like a jackrabbit in my chest. I wish to God I had the bullets. I have to make him think that the rifle is loaded or I'm doomed. "I'm warning you, mister, stay the hell back."

The man's smile gets wider. "You gonna shoot me, son? An innocent man looking for a little sup? That's right unneighbourly of you."

I keep the rifle aimed at his head. The man coughs out a wheezing, whisky laugh and scrubs at his stubble. "You know what I think?" he says. "I think you ain't got the guts to pull that trigger."

I cock the rifle and grip it tighter.

He squints at me, sizing up the situation. He licks his lips as though pondering a great riddle. "Maybe you're all show and no go, you know what I mean? Maybe you got no bullets in that gun at' all."

My heart skips a beat as he says this and my eyes betray me.

"Hoohoo! I was right!" He gives a little skip and dance. Then he puts his hands on his hips and cocks his head to one side, his face darkening. "I'm going to have that saddle, son, and all the rest of your things."

He lunges, grabbing Lazy Boy by the muzzle and knocking me to the ground. He stands over me, a twisted silhouette, raising the rifle in the air. My mind is a whirling slot machine of pictures and words. The man grins as he swings, the rifle carving an arc like a hatchet blade through the air.

All of a sudden I hear a shout and the crack of wood against stone. Smokey rears and whinnies. The rifle clatters to the ground as the man falls, hollering and screaming and pounding. I roll safely to one side and look up to see the dog tearing the man to pieces. It's snarling and snapping like the devil unleashed, its flashing teeth proclaiming the most terrible kind of judgment. The man screams and tries to run, but the dog drags him back down and goes to work. There's blood, lots of it, and I hope that it isn't the dog's, as the man kicks and punches for his life.

"Call it off! Call it off!"

I stay where I am. I can't believe what I'm seeing. The man staggers to his feet and stumbles away, the dog ripping at his pants as he hops and limps through the meadow. He falls and rises and falls again, the dog chasing him fiendishly, until they disappear over a small hill and are gone.

In the canopy high overhead, the cicadas begin to buzz. The breeze whispers. The leaves rustle. I reach for Lazy Boy. There's a dent on the butt of the rifle where it smashed against the stones. I go to stand but my legs give way and Lazy Boy tumbles to my feet. Throat burning, I collapse, face buried in my hands. I want to cry—I *have* to cry—but the tears won't come. So I just sit there, shaking and shuddering, the taste of snot and sweat in my mouth. I sit like this for what seems like a very long time, until I feel a small nudge on my back.

"Smokey." I throw my arms around his neck. He smells so familiar, so good and right that the tears come at last, running hot and salty down my cheeks.

I'm still holding Smokey when I see a black shape zigzagging along through the meadow grass. It's the dog, coming back. He reaches the edge of the woods and lies down on the periphery of the camp, the way he did before. This reminds me that I've forgotten about the beans. I pull them from the fire and check the damage. One side of the pot is a little scorched, but the rest is fine. I look at the dog. It pants heavily, staring off into the woods like nothing has happened, as though nearly killing someone is all in a day's work. My stomach lurches at the thought of the man. As hungry as I am, I can't bring myself to eat the beans. In fact, I don't think I'll ever be able to eat beans again. Besides, the dog deserves them more than I do. Finding a flat rock, I rinse it off in the river. I scrape the beans from the pot onto the rock with my spoon, letting them sit until they're cool, before placing them on the ground, halfway between me and the dog. Then I crouch near the fire and wait.

The dog glances at my gift from the corner of his eye, not sure if it's a trick. I can't blame him. I've been throwing rocks and flaming logs at him the whole time to keep him away from the food, and now I'm offering up a whole can of beans, no questions asked.

"Come on," I say, trying to encourage him.

He looks at me warily.

"Come on, boy." I give a little whistle.

There is a look of recognition in his eyes. He stands.

"That's it. Come and get it. Maple beans, the best there is."

He takes a few steps forward, watching me the whole time. I stay crouched down, so as not to frighten him. It seems kind of funny, him being afraid of me when I've seen what he can do. It just makes me respect him all the more. At last, when he can fight his desire no longer, he approaches the rock. He doesn't even sniff before he gobbles the beans down, licking the stone until it glistens.

"Good boy," I say. Smokey thinks I'm talking to him and steps over to me, nuzzling my back. "You're good too, Smokes. But Dog is the real hero today. Right, Dog?" I pull a corn dodger from my shirt and break it into pieces. Dog looks at me expectantly. I toss a few bits, narrowing the distance between us. He pads up to the dodger and eats it, then looks up for more. I toss another piece, and another, talking gently the whole time, until he is about five or six feet away and the dodger is gone.

"No more, buddy." I show him my empty hands, then slowly rise to my feet. Dog lowers himself to the ground, panting. We both seem pleased with the headway we've made.

Dog watches from the shade of the mulberry bush while I break camp and prepare Smokey for the second leg of the day's trip. I whistle when we're ready to go. He gets up and trots along behind us, staying about ten feet back. Grabbing a Pop-Tart from the saddlebags, I toss him a piece. He bolts it down and continues to follow along, keeping an even, loping pace, his tongue lolling, eyes focused forward. Just this morning I was cursing his hide and now I'm luring him to stick around. But I feel safer knowing a dog like him is standing guard.

After an hour or two I stop to check the compass and adjust our course. I have no idea how far we've come from. We eventually meet with a set of train tracks that point in the desired direction so I follow them. As we ride along in the ditch beside the tracks, my mind starts remembering. It takes me to a time years ago when Cid and I used to ride our horse Sep along the rail lines. We were just little kids, barely enough weight between the two of us to make up a sack of flour. Sep was a mountain pony, sturdy and faithful. Completely black except for a small white star in the centre of his forehead. He could drink pop straight from the can, gripping it with his teeth and tilting his head back. We loved to watch him do it. He was a good pony, full of loyalty and trust. Even after he went blind, he let us ride him, galloping full out if we asked him to.

We used to race trains back then, running in the ditch to the cut-off where the grass disappeared and the stone cliff jumped up against the rails. It was a dangerous game because there was always the fear that we wouldn't make it and that we would get crushed between the train and the cliff face. We usually gave ourselves a good head start, but there was one time when a locomotive caught us off guard. It barrelled down on us, whistle shrieking. Sep bolted straight to a gallop and we hollered him on, tearing along the ditch as the train roared closer and closer. I remember Cid shouting in my ear to go faster, and then the sudden feeling of weightlessness as we somersaulted through the air. Sep had hit a hole and pitched us. He landed inches from me as I crashed, Cid smashing on top of me. But old Sep scrambled up and continued to run as we gaped helplessly from the ground. He raced along the ditch, stone blind, beating the train to the cut-off and veering up the slope into the woods toward home. We found him later, standing peacefully at the edge of the woods, waiting for us to come and get him.

I laugh out loud as I remember this, making Smokey and Dog look up at me. I start to whistle to pass the time. *"Frère Jacques."* My companions seem to enjoy it. Smokey twists his ears back and forth with interest. Dog winks with a kind of canine smile in his eyes.

We follow the tracks until the woods give way to backlots and the beginnings of a small town. There's little more than a few tired houses, an old train station and a dingy variety store with a dinged-up Neilson ice cream sign. It's so unremarkable, it could be any town, anywhere. I'm just hoping they really do sell ice cream and a whole lot more. I tie Smokey to a bike rack, cover Lazy Boy with my jacket and dump the flattened cans in the garbage. Dog flops in the only bit of shade at the corner of the store.

A muted bell rings as I enter the shop. The light is dim and dusty after the blinding glare of the sun. There seems to be no one here. A TV flickers on the wall to one side of the counter. The shelves are practically bare except for a smattering of sun-faded goods straight out of the sixties. There's no ice cream in sight, either. The freezers are all broken and secured with duct tape. There are old boxes of Pop-Tarts though. They look like the first pastries Kellogg's ever made. They don't even have icing on them. Still, beggars can't be choosers. The strawberry and blueberry don't look too bad so I take a box of each. I pass right by the beans and choose several cans of Alphagetti, some Chef Boyardee ravioli and some Campbell's SpaghettiOs with meatballs. There's a small metal garden trowel that I decide to get, thinking it will be good for digging toilet holes, and a whole package of Red Bird matches, four boxes to a pack. I pick up a toothbrush, a couple of cans of dog food (the kind with vegetables and real meat gravy), some ChapStick and a two-roll of toilet paper. I carry the lot to the front of the store and drop it on the counter, where I peruse the candy. I can't believe they actually have licorice pipes and Big Turks. Who eats those? They don't have my favourite chocolate bars: Reese's Peanut Butter Cups and Crispy Crunch. Only Snickers, Mars and Kit Kat. Big Turks don't even count as chocolate.

They do carry Big Red chewing gum, I'm happy to see. I grab the last three packs left in the display box.

While I'm deliberating over the chocolate, a woman with a face as hard as a shovel blade shuffles into the shop from some room in the back. She has a cigarette sticking out of her mouth—no doubt a permanent fixture—cat-eye glasses as old as the Pop-Tarts and one of those dressing gowns worn by grandmothers everywhere that aren't really meant to be seen in public. She nods at my groceries and squints at me through the cigarette smoke.

"That it?"

"Uhm . . . no . . . I want some candy." I grab several Snickers, a couple Kit Kats, a Mars bar, a couple more Kit Kats and some butterscotch Lifesavers. "That's it."

The woman begins to ring my order through on an antique cash register where the numbers pop up with each purchase. I'm watching the tally to be sure she's adding it correctly when I notice something on the TV. It's a newscast showing a recent school photo of me with the word "Missing" emblazoned overtop. There's no sound so I have no idea what's being said, but it's clear that I'm in big trouble. The woman notices me staring at the screen and turns her head in time to catch a glimpse of my picture before the image flickers to something else. When she looks at me again, it's through different eyes. Her voice takes on a forced pleasant tone.

"You going camping?"

I shake my head no, then nod yes. The woman stares at me suspiciously. I see her hand reach under the counter. I think maybe she's pushing a button to call the police. The total on the cash register is $16.73. I toss $17 on the counter and dismiss the change.

"I don't need a bag," I say, gathering up the groceries in my arms and making for the door. I hit it with my shoulder but it doesn't open. *Pull.* I hook one finger over the bar on the door and yank, dropping a Snickers and a pack of gum to the floor. The woman doesn't try to help me. She just watches from behind the counter as I fling the door open, kicking the candy out as I go. There's a group of kids loitering around Smokey, their faces as hard as the one on the woman in the store. Dog is standing nervously in the shadow of the building. A grubby little kid has his hands on Lazy Boy.

"Don't touch that!"

The kids don't even bother to move as I walk up and start slinging food into the saddlebags every which way. I just want to get out of here. I unhitch Smokey and mount, whistling for Dog. The woman pokes her head out of the store. One of the kids picks up the Snickers and gum and hands it to me.

"Keep it," I say, kicking Smokey into a canter. Dog takes up the rear, running easily. He didn't even need to be told to come along.

I can feel the eyes of those kids and that woman staring at us as we clatter across the street and dip over the tracks. Once again I'm on the run. The only difference is, last time it was just the local radio station out looking for me. This time the whole province has been alerted. For all I know, the whole country too. I have to call Queenie and Cid to let them know that I'm all right. I'm sure there was a phone booth back at the variety. But I won't be able to return until after dark or I'll get caught. I wonder briefly if any of this has to do with the hobo that tried to rob us. What if he's dead and Dog and I are suspects?

We canter along the rails until the little town fades away to trees and fields. We ride deep into the woods, me looking back repeatedly to be sure that no one has followed us and that we're hidden from view. A shady opening beckons. We stop to rest. I set up camp, forgoing the fire because the smoke might attract attention. I let Smokey graze, and I feed Dog one of the cans of food. He gobbles it down, then finds a spot to rest and wait for what's next. I eat a Snickers and one of the remaining cinnamon Pop-Tarts. I'm still ravenous so I open a can of SpaghettiOs and eat them cold, right out of the can. There's not much difference between Dog and me now, I think.

I call him over, just to see if he'll come. He walks over to me, his head hung in submission. I reach out my hand to let him sniff it. He does this for a long while then takes a step closer. I talk gently to him as I stroke his head. He closes his eyes in appreciation. He's a nice-looking dog, really. With a bath and some good groom-ing, he'd almost be beautiful. But there's something wild about him that no amount of soap and water can wash away. His eyes are gold with a savage glint at the corners. His paws are big as saucers and his canines are long and curved. He's part wolf, there's no doubt about that now that I've seen him up close. I wonder if he could ever be tame enough to be comfortable around people the way a normal dog can. I'm not even sure if I can trust him completely.

I get Smokey's comb from my kit and softly brush Dog's fur. He seems to enjoy the feeling and even lets me pick a couple of burrs from his tail. But I don't pester him too much for now. I want him to get used to the idea of being handled before I tackle the harder stuff. I'm not sure how Ma will react when I bring him home. I'll have to convince her that he's good and that he's worth keep-ing, the same way I did with Smokey. A lump forms in my throat when I think of Ma lying in that hospital bed.

Does she even know that I'm missing and that the police are looking for me? I wonder who called the cops this time. I don't think Queenie or Cid would do it. It may have been the rumpled man from the Children's Aid. In any case, it doesn't matter at this point.

Dog leans his shoulder against me. He seems to understand what I'm feeling inside. He places his big head in my lap, as gentle as a kitten, and licks my hand. Smokey grazes nearby, foraging peacefully in the diminishing light. Looking over our little ragtag crew, I can't help thinking that we're all just a bunch of misfits, Dog, Smokey and me.

chapter 17
death comes knocking

By the time it's good and dark, I'm ready to risk going back into town. It wouldn't make sense to ride Smokey right up to the variety store. I'll have to tether him someplace safe from prying eyes, yet close enough for a quick getaway. I'm also thinking that I should disguise myself. But how? And then I remember Dad's uniform in the knapsack. It's a kooky idea but it just might work. No one is going to be looking for a young soldier. They're looking for a kid in jeans and a T-shirt.

I dig the uniform out and try it on. It's a bit big, but not by much. Dad was fifteen when he entered the Merchant Marines, only two years older than me. I marvel at his bravery as I roll the pants and sleeves up at the cuff. I wish I had a mirror so I could see myself. The wool is hot and scratchy against my skin. Smokey and Dog watch with interest as I fasten the brass buttons on the coat. Smokey is especially curious when I start to saddle him up. Dog doesn't seem to care what we do. He's ready for anything at all times.

We pick our way carefully along the railway tracks toward town. The idea of going back has me feeling skittish as a young colt. I'm sure that woman at the variety store would turn me over to the police for a dime if she thought they'd pay it. I don't like riding at night either. Anyone could be hiding out in the woods beside the tracks, though I'm confident Dog would let me know about it. Strangely, I've never heard him bark, but I'm sure he's not about to let someone catch me unawares again.

It seems to take a very long time to get to the point in the tracks where we left the variety store behind. Nothing looks familiar. I survey the sky. The stars shimmer brightly and I can see the dusty expanse of the Milky Way reclining overhead. The moon is a sickle blade of silver. Everything is so clear and crisp it hardly looks real at all. It looks more like the simulated sky I saw once on a school trip to the planetarium, where they recreated the moon and stars and everything by shining a lamp through a piece of black paper punched with holes. I wonder if there are other planets with people on them, looking up at their own sky in a similar way. For some reason, thinking about this makes me feel completely alone.

The tracks stretch into the darkness and I'm starting to lose my cool when all at once the trees part and I see

the store, lit up by a lone street lamp. It's closed for the
night. The rest of the town is dead too. There's no one
out. I'm relieved to see the phone booth, tucked against
one corner of the building. I rein Smokey around and
double back along the rails. I find a good spot to tie him,
far enough from the tracks to be safe but close enough
that I can reach him in a hurry if need be. I think to
bring Lazy Boy, then decide against it. A boy carrying
a gun would look suspicious no matter what the situation, military uniform or not. Dog waits as I secure
Smokey's lead to a tree branch. I tell him to sit and stay
but he just looks blankly back at me.

"All right, come on then," I say, because I know he's
just going to follow me anyway.

We creep along the tracks toward the light. I check
up and down the street before crossing. It's as though
they dropped a neutron bomb on the place it's so quiet.
Dog and I stroll up to the store, like we have every right
to be there. When we reach the phone booth, Dog
stands to one side in the shadows. He doesn't like to
be seen.

I lift the receiver from the cradle and check my pants
pockets for coins. But my pockets are empty. I've left
all my change in my jeans. It doesn't matter anyway,
because when I hold the phone to my ear there's no
dial tone. I inspect the line and discover that it's not

even connected to the rest of the phone. Some goof yanked it out at the roots. I slam the phone into its cradle. Dog steps into the light, licking his lips nervously. He's looking past me to a spot somewhere down the street. I follow his line of vision and see a gang of boys approaching. They don't look friendly. Stepping from the booth, I walk as nonchalantly as possible, hands in my pockets.

"Hey!" one of the boys yells out.

I ignore him, picking up the pace.

"Hey!" the guy calls again.

I'm inclined to run but decide against it, turning to face the gang. Dog presses against my leg.

"What do you think you're doing?"

The gang moves closer. There are five of them, all about fifteen or sixteen. They're dressed pretty much the same: jeans, untied sneakers and blue baseball caps. Except for the leader, whose cap is red.

"I asked you a question, sailor boy," he says.

I actually forgot that I'm wearing Dad's uniform. "I was just walking," I say.

Red Cap looks at his friends in astonishment. "He was just walking. Who said you could walk here, doofus?"

"I didn't know I needed permission."

He grabs one of his friends by the shirt collar. "He

didn't know he needed permission." The friend smiles stupidly. He's not going to argue. Red Cap looks at me, his eyes angry slits glittering from beneath the brim of his hat. "I own this town," he says. "And everything in it. That makes you a trespasser. And you know what we do with trespassers?" He releases his friend and steps forward. Dog curls his lips over his teeth and growls.

"I haven't a clue," I say, emboldened by Dog's display. "But me and my dog would surely like to know."

The guy looks at Dog and smirks, but he doesn't take another step. Dog growls a little louder. "I'll tell you what," he says. "Why don't you and your mutt go back to your ship, or wherever it is you came from, and we'll forget all about it." He punches his fist in his hand.

Dog snaps and snarls when he does this.

"I'll tell *you* what," I say, wishing Cid were here to witness this moment. "Why don't you and your friends take a hike, and Dog and I will forget we ever saw you."

The muscles jump in Red Cap's jaw and his friends shift uncomfortably behind him. There's a long moment where he and I just stare at each other, but then one of his sidekicks pipes up in the background.

"Hey, it's him . . ." he says.

His friends look around.

The guy points to me. "It's him—the kid from the TV! The one everybody is looking for."

"I don't know what you're talking about," I say.

"It's him, I tell you," the guy persists. "He's the kid from the news!"

"Isn't there some kind of reward for finding him?" another guy says.

"Yeah yeah yeah, I think so. Come on! The cops are gonna love us for this." They light out down the street.

Red Cap smiles and points his finger at me. "You are in so much trouble, kid." He thumps his fist in his hand again and takes off after his friends.

Dog lunges at him but I run in the other direction and he quickly whips around to follow me. We tear across the street and along the tracks to where Smokey is tied. I undo the lead in record time and in seconds we're galloping along the tracks, stones flying, Dog an invisible blur beside us. I'm afraid that Smokey will stumble in the dark but I urge him on all the same. If old Sep could race trains stone blind, I'm praying that Smokey can keep his footing with a little light from the moon. We hit a soft patch of gravel and Smokey's hind legs slip, but he gathers himself and we keep running.

The wall of forest suddenly opens up and I take the opportunity to leave the tracks and enter the woods. We skid down the embankment and up the ditch to the other side, slowing to a trot. I can't risk making camp, not with those kids calling the cops and all, so we push through the night. For the most part it's easy going until we hit a river. It's not a creek or a winding river like before. It's wide and fast, glowing like a highway of phosphorescent ink through the trees. We go up and down the bank, searching for a place to cross. I think to go back to the tracks and cross the river that way, but I have no idea how far we've come since entering the woods. I rein Smokey around and we pick our way west along the shore. The river only gets wider. We'll have to cross soon or we'll be stuck.

We reach a sandy spot where the water seems to slow. I kick Smokey on. He balks, then splashes in. I give him his head. He nickers nervously, but the bottom holds and we're crossing well. Dog wades in after us. I whistle him on and he dives in, paddling through the inky liquid. The water level remains steady, cresting at Smokey's knees. I'm watching our progress, the Milky Way reflected on the surface, my own shadow undulating along as we advance. And then we drop.

For a moment we're both under water. There is a muffled silence before we surface, Smokey snorting and splashing, and me choking and shouting. At first I'm worried about the water ruining all my things: Lazy Boy and Dad's uniform, my food and clothes. Until I realize that we could die. The force of the river drags us downstream. It pulls us along like driftwood, sucking us under. Smokey struggles, fighting to keep his head. I let myself slip from the saddle and clutch the saddlebags, praying that Smokey is strong enough to swim us both to shore. The wool uniform becomes a shroud with the weight of the water. My backpack is a boulder dragging me down. I free one arm, then the other, the dark fingers of the river snatching up the bag and everything in it, except the words of Robert Frost's poem. They stay in my head, goading me on. *And miles to go before I sleep.* The riverbank is so far away. We kick and fight. I don't know where Dog is. All at once, the shore seems closer, and I think that we may make it after all. But something snags my leg and I'm torn away from Smokey. Arms flailing, I twirl and twist, tossed like a leaf on the water. I have no air. There is no air to have. I see Smokey, scrabbling up the bank on the other side. Then everything goes black.

★ ★ ★

I am aware of two things: the sun beating down on my face and the sound of birds singing over the rushing of water. I'm still in the river, I know that, but somehow I'm alive. I open my eyes and try to move but I can't. My skull feels like it's split in half and I seem to be tangled up in the branches of a tree. There's blood dripping into my eyes.

I turn my head as best I can. Smokey is standing patiently on the riverbank, blinking back at me. Dog is pacing anxiously along the water. He steps into the river and whines. I try to untangle myself but the pain swells in my head and everything goes black again.

* * *

When my eyes open next I'm struck by the oddest image. Both Smokey and Dog are in front of me, staring at something in the woods. At first I think it's a deer. Then I see that it's a girl. Dog's hackles are up and he's growling. I try to motion to the girl but can only watch helplessly as she disappears among the trees. The river tugs at my legs. Mosquitoes buzz in my ears and bite my face. Slow drops of blood hit my hand in red starbursts that trickle down my fingers and drip into the water. Dog and Smokey continue to stare into the woods while birds chatter in the trees. The pain in my head rises and falls.

Eventually, the girl reappears. She crouches down, one hand outstretched, and remains motionless for the longest time. Does she even see me? I fade in and out, but each time I open my eyes, Dog is one step closer to the girl. I want to call out to her, to let her know that I'm hurt. I open my mouth to yell but a moan comes out instead.

Then the girl is beside me. She's standing in the water, pulling on my coat. All at once my legs and arms spring free and I drop into the river with a splash. The girl turns me over and holds me under the arms, struggling to drag me to dry ground. When we're safely on the riverbank, she bends down and speaks into my ear. "Everything is going to be all right," she says.

Dog licks my face as the girl sets about gathering long tree branches. I think she's building a fire but then she takes the branches and begins binding them with rope. I'm curious about what she's doing but the pain in my head won't let me stay awake. I drift off, I don't know for how long, and when I come to again, the girl has me under the arms once more, is pulling me into a stretcher-like thing that she's made from the branches and harnessed to Smokey. She has to work hard to get me up into the contraption and I want to tell her to stop, it hurts too much. She ties me with a piece of rope to the stretcher. Smokey stands by patiently.

"He's a good boy," I try to tell her.

I don't think she hears me because she disappears again. Then we begin to move, lurching and trundling over the ground. Dog trots beside me. I reach to pet him and my arm flops over the side of the stretcher. The grass runs through my fingers.

The next thing I know, I'm beneath blankets on a

mattress in a small cabin. My clothes are in a heap on the floor. The girl sits next to me. She chews something and spits it into her hand then presses it to my forehead. I can't stop my body from shaking as she wraps my head with a piece of cloth. I want to tell her that I'm sorry as she climbs in next to me and holds me until the shaking stops.

After a while she tells me that she must go. "I have to get help," she says.

I don't want her to leave. My mouth opens and closes like a goldfish's but no words come out. She must think that I'm thirsty, because she holds a canteen of water to my lips then tucks the blankets around me. Dog lies on the floor beside the mattress.

"I will be back as soon as I can," the girl says. "I promise."

It seems like she's gone forever. While she's away, my body starts to shake more violently than before and my mind plays tricks on me. I see things that don't make sense, images from long ago, of Dad and Ma, Queenie and Cid. The old lady from the hospital appears too. She stands in the doorway, smiling and nodding the way she did in the Emergency, before slowly fading from view. It makes me sad to see her go. I am thinking that the girl has left me to die out here in the woods when all at once I hear voices. Dog jumps up and growls as two men step through the doorway. The girl is with them. She holds Dog so the men can tend to me. They speak in a familiar language that I don't understand as they lift me, mattress and all, and I can't help but cry out with pain. They carry me to a truck that is waiting on a road in the forest and place me in the back. The girl gets in beside me.

"What's your name?" I manage to ask as she takes my hand.

She smiles, sunlight streaming around her face. "Raven," she says.

* * *

I wake to the sound of a mechanized *beep*. I am in a room, the walls as white as the sunlight pouring through the window. The *beep* sounds again. The hospital. I'm in the hospital. Ma must need her IV changed. I rise to get the nurse. A terrible pain erupts in my head. My tongue is dry and heavy as lead. I feel all woozy and the room shifts as though loose on its hinges. A cool hand reaches for mine.

"You must stay in bed."

It's the girl, Raven. She's sitting on a chair next to me.

I lie back down. She pulls the sheet over my chest.

"The nurse is coming," she says. Her voice is light and rich with accent.

"Where am I?" I ask.

"The hospital. In Belle River. You've had an accident."

"An accident?" And then it all comes rushing back to me: the river, Smokey struggling to swim, the water, pulling me down. "What about Smokey and Dog?" I say, trying to get up again.

Raven coaxes me back down. "They are fine. I have taken care of them."

I reach to touch my head. It's bandaged, and so is my hand. I feel so groggy. I can barely focus my eyes, but when I do, I can't help staring at Raven. Her skin is smooth, the colour of toffee, and her hair is black as ebony. It shimmers like the feathers of a crow. Her eyes are gold in the light. They sparkle with kindness.

"You're the one who helped me," I say.

"Yes. I found you at the edge of the river. You were snagged by a tree. Are you a soldier?"

I think about this for a minute and remember Dad's uniform. I turn to see it folded neatly on the bedside table. The watch is there too, but the crystal is smashed. It must have gotten broken in the river.

"How long have I been here?"

"Three days."

My eyes widen.

"Everything is fine," Raven says. "Your dog and your horse have been staying with me."

"Smokey," I say, looking up at her.

Our eyes lock and I am flooded with images of her taking care of me. I remember her holding me to stop the shaking, her skin soft and warm against mine. The colour rises in my face when I conclude that she has seen me naked.

"My pony," I start to explain. "His name is Smokey."

"He is a good horse," she says. "Why were you running away?"

"I wasn't running . . . I was looking . . . for my father."

She nods, as though this is perfectly natural. "Your father is coming."

"What? Here?" I raise myself on one elbow but the pain explodes in my head, forcing me back down on the pillow.

"The nurse said that he called and that he is coming to take you home. He saw you on the TV."

"When will he be here?"

Raven shakes her head. "He didn't say exactly, only that he is coming."

"What about Ma? And Queenie and Cid?" I ask.

Raven shakes her head again. "I don't know."

"My ma is sick," I start to tell her, just as the nurse bustles into the room. She smiles at me as she checks the IV, replacing the bag with a new one. Then she inspects the bandage on my head.

"You've had quite the adventure, eh?" the nurse says.

"Do you know anything about my ma?" I ask, as she takes my wrist to check my pulse.

"We called your family when you were admitted," she says, placing my arm back down on the bed. "Your mother is doing much better. But you can call home for yourself when you're feeling up to it."

I'm so relieved to hear this, I could cry. I want to know more but the nurse seems to be in a hurry. She clatters around the room, doing this and that, then leaves as quickly as she came.

I turn to Raven. "There was a rifle . . ."

"Lazy Boy, yes. You spoke of it. My father likes this gun. He says it is very old and worth a lot of money. It is with the rest of your things."

"I lost my backpack."

"We did not find it. The river is fast."

"Your name is Raven," I say, like some kind of blithering idiot.

"Yes," she says, with gentleness. "And you are Nathaniel Howard Estabrooks from Eastview, Ontario."

All at once I understand that her accent is French. She is Métis. I feel ashamed that she can speak my language perfectly and I know only a few words of hers. "You found me by the river."

"The Thames, yes. I found you snagged on a log," she says. "That's how your uniform got torn. Your head was bleeding—from a rock, I think."

I shudder as I remember the cold, dark hands of the river. "I thought I was going to drown," I say. "I thought all of us were going to."

"Horses and dogs are good swimmers," Raven says. "They are faithful too. They protected you. Smokey stood beside you the whole time. And your dog. He didn't want me to come near at first."

"I hope you didn't have any trouble with him," I say, remembering what Dog did to the hobo.

Raven smiles her beautiful smile. "He is a marshmallow for food. I fed him little bits on the ground, then fed him from my hand like this."

She crouches down on the floor, her hand outstretched, making little noises of encouragement with her mouth.

"He's a sucker for that," I say, and I have to laugh, thinking about Dog being lured again by that trick.

Raven laughs too. "He is my best friend now," she says.

I point to the bandage on my head. "When you were dressing my wounds . . . you put something on them. And that stretcher that you made . . . how did you know to do that?"

Raven nods. "I used a plant called yarrow to stop the bleeding. It is a traditional remedy. The stretcher is called a travois. I made it from branches and rope, in the old way. I know that it was not so comfortable, but it was the only thing I could do because you were in no condition to ride your pony."

"I was shaking . . ." I say.

"Yes," she agrees. "I held you until the shaking stopped. I was afraid that you would die."

She lowers her eyes when she says this, so as not to betray her emotions, I think. This makes me like her even more.

"But I didn't die," I stupidly say.

"No. You are here, talking to me." She raises her eyes to look at me, and my heart turns to putty.

"Because of you," I say. "I owe my life to you."

"We all worked together to save you," she says. "Dog, Smokey, my brother and father, and me."

"I'd like to thank your father and brother some time."

"You can do that soon," Raven says. "They think you were brave to ride your horse into the woods alone."

"Smokey's a good boy," I say.

"Yes, he is. I rode him to go get help. He ran hard."

I imagine Raven, galloping on Smokey through the forest to her home. She must have looked like a queen with her dark hair flying. "Belle River," I say. "That's near Windsor."

"You were very close to the border. You almost made it."

"But I wanted to cross at Sarnia," I say. "At Moosetown or Courtright. My compass must have been off for me to stray so far south."

"You came a long way."

Just then, the nurse reappears. She injects something with a needle into the IV tube. She tells me that my X-rays look good and that it shouldn't be long before I can go home, but for now I must rest.

Raven stands as though to leave. Something comes over me and I grab her hand. I'm not ready to be alone. She looks at the nurse, who indicates that she can stay, then she leans over and does the most surprising thing. She kisses me, on the lips, lightly, and soft as a butterfly's wings. Then she sits back in the chair, holding my hand in her lap. My heart skips wildly. I want to kiss her again, but I can only gaze at her as the medicine swirls through me.

chapter 18
a new beginning

The first thing I see when I open my eyes the next day is Raven. She's sitting in the chair next to me, as though she never left.

"Did you go home?" I ask.

"Of course," she says. "But I am back. Look—I have a present for you."

She reaches her hand into the pocket of her vest and pulls out a tiny piece of blue sky. "A robin's egg," she says, placing it gently in my hand.

I examine the egg. It weighs almost nothing. "It's beautiful," I say. "Will it hatch?"

"No. It is too late in the season."

I stretch my hand out to give it back to her but she closes my fingers around the egg. "It's for you," she says. "It's a gift."

I look at the egg again. It's so perfect, so completely innocent and vulnerable that it makes me want to cry. It's so fragile, and yet it's hopeful too. "Thank you," I say, placing the egg carefully on the table next to the bed so that it won't fall off and break. "My sister Queenie will love it."

"Tell me about your family," Raven says.

"What do you want to know?"

"Tell me everything," she says.

And so I do. I tell Raven as much as I can. It's hard for me to stay awake. The pain in my head is too much for me and the medicine makes me so tired. But when I'm not sleeping, or being fussed over by the nurses, I entertain Raven with tales of the three of us kids getting into so much trouble. I tell her about Ma, and Dad too. Not just the sad things, about him leaving and how hard it's been for all of us, but the nice things as well: the skating rinks he used to make in the backyard and the magic tricks he used to perform to entertain us when we were little. She smiles at most of my stories, but gets all serious when I mention the fire in Ted Henry's barn, or poor old Jed, the horse who died when his neck was broken by a falling beam. She thinks I'm brave to have run away from the man and his son who wanted to buy Smokey, and she makes me tell that particular story over again.

When I'm too exhausted to talk, Raven tells me about her life. She speaks of her mother, who is long since gone, and her father and brother, who still trap and hunt for a living. She tells me about the medicinal plants in the woods, how they heal, and about the spirits that inhabit them. But my favourite stories are the ones where she talks about the old ways, handed down to her from her great-grandparents in songs and traditional dances.

Spending time with Raven, I'm amazed at how easy it is to talk to her, though my blood races whenever I look into her face. It eventually occurs to me that I feel as comfortable around Raven as I felt awkward around Alyson and the other girls from the stable. I know now that I shouldn't have felt so out of place at Tanglewood. Some of it was my fault, really, because I have to be okay with who I am, no matter what the situation. Raven helps me to understand that. She says that I should be myself and be proud to be a good person, whether I ride like a cowboy or not. She says you can't put a price on human dignity and decency, and that it takes all kinds of people to make the world go around—and I agree.

The whole day, Raven doesn't leave my side. She helps me eat, tells me stories, sits patiently in the chair next to the bed as I drift in and out of sleep. She even stays when the police arrive, asking questions. They speak to me, then Raven, writing notes and talking to the nurses before they leave. They don't ask about the hobo, I'm glad to say.

After dinner, Raven says that she has a surprise for me. She calls for the nurse, who appears with a wheelchair. Raven helps me into the chair and covers my legs with a blanket, then rolls me to the elevators at the end of the hall.

"Where are we going?" I ask, but Raven just shakes her head and smiles.

"It's a surprise," she tells me again as we get into the elevator and ride to the ground floor.

Once there, Raven pushes me to the main entrance at the front of the hospital and out the sliding doors.

"Close your eyes, and don't open them until I say," she tells me.

I close my eyes, and when I open them again, Raven is standing next to me, Dog at her side. He's all bathed and groomed and he looks amazing. He's even wearing a new leather collar. He wags his tail excitedly. He's so happy to see me, he practically climbs into my lap.

"How did you do this?" I ask, scrubbing Dog's head.

"My father dropped him off," Raven says. "He's gone to find a parking spot. We would have brought Smokey, too, but he wouldn't fit into the truck."

We laugh at this.

"But how did you manage to bathe him?" I ask.

"I told you. He is my best friend now."

I look at Dog in wonder, then up at Raven. "This is the nicest thing anyone has ever done for me." I fidget with the brass tag on the collar, blinking back the tears that well in my eyes.

Raven looks at me thoughtfully. "You should name him," she says.

Of course she's right. He should have a name, especially if I'm going to keep him. I have no idea how he'll manage in our tiny apartment, and I don't know what Ma's going to think, but I just can't leave him behind or give him to someone else after all we've been through.

"I don't know what to call him," I say.

"How about Bandit," Raven suggests.

"Bandit?"

"Yes, you know, like Smokey and the Bandit."

I burst out laughing, inciting Dog to jump right into my lap, a mischievous little smile in his eyes. "He likes it," I say.

Raven leans over and ruffles Bandit's fur. He licks her face and she hugs him. I can't believe what a teddy bear he's become. He's so big he's practically pushing me out of the wheelchair, but I don't mind. I'm just happy to see him. I turn to Raven and our eyes meet. We stare at each other for a long time, until her father appears.

He's a huge man with long dark hair like Raven's. He stretches out his hand to me and I take it.

"I want to thank you for everything you did for me," I say.

He nods and smiles. "I'm glad to see that you are feeling better."

* * *

It's nearly dark by the time Raven and her father leave with Bandit. I'm sad to see them go but I've been waiting for a chance to call home and this seems like a good time.

Queenie answers the phone. She turns into a blubbering mess the second she hears my voice.

"Oh, Nat," she cries. "We thought you were gone for good."

"I'm fine," I say. "Everything is going to be okay now."

"*I'm* the one who found your note," she sniffs. "Cid and I ran to the barn but you and Smokey were already gone. We were so worried. And so was Alyson. She told us that she talked to you before you left. She said that she was scared for you and that we should tell somebody. Cid called Ma's boss, Mr. McKinley, because she didn't know who else to talk to, and he said it was best to tell the police. I hope you're not mad. Alyson was just trying to help."

"It's okay, Queenie," I say. "I'm not mad at anyone. You guys did the right thing."

At these words, Queenie breaks down again. "When are you coming home?" she asks between sobs. "We bought a new can opener."

This makes me laugh, but Queenie just keeps crying. And then Cid takes the phone. But she's crying too. Then I'm crying, the words catching in my throat.

"Ma's going to be all right," Cid manages to say through her tears. "She's actually sitting up a little, and she's starting to eat real food again. She asks about you, Nat—every day."

I nod into the phone. Now I'm the one having trouble speaking.

"Charlie Chaplin from the Children's Aid returned, just like you said he would," Cid continues. "But Mr. McKinley helped out. He took care of things so that we can all stay together. He gave us money and even arranged for a housekeeper until Ma gets better."

Hearing this makes me respect and admire Mr. McKinley, and I regret anything I may have said in the past about him being cheap. I make a silent vow to go see him after I get home. When I finally find my voice, I assure Cid that Smokey is fine. I tell her about Bandit, and about my adventure, though I don't say a word about the hobo. I do tell her about Raven, though. I can't hide the emotion in my voice, no matter how I try. But Cid doesn't let on. Instead she gets all quiet, her voice so small I can barely hear her.

"Nat . . ." she says. "Will you promise me one thing? Promise that you will never leave again. We're a family, Nat, and we can work things out together, no matter how bad it gets."

She sounds so much like Ma, talking like this, that I promise I will never leave her and Queenie again. I tell her that I love her and that I miss her and that I can't wait to get home. She tells me that she loves me too.

And then she asks about Dad.

* * *

I've had a shower and I'm sitting up in bed. The nurse has changed my bandages and has made me look as presentable as possible. My eye is the colour of a plum and my ribs are bruised as old apples. The pain in my head has been dulled by medicine.

I can't believe that Dad is coming to take me home. After years of wondering and waiting, it turns out that Cid was right: he does live in Illinois. He's driving to Belle River to pick me up, the nurse said, and he's even bringing a little trailer to haul Smokey, so we can take him home too.

Raven waits with me. She's wearing a red flowered

dress and sandals. Her hair is pulled back with a silver clip, but it can't be tamed so easily. It falls in loose strands around her face as she presses my hand to her heart.

"Promise that you'll write to me," she says.

My own heart aches in the strangest way, like it's growing too big for my chest. I want to take a picture of her, sitting in her flowered dress, her dark hair tumbling down. I want to tell her the way I feel. I try to find the words to express how much she means to me and how happy I am that she found me. But none of it comes out right. I just blather and stumble along until she unclasps her hair and stops my talking with a kiss. Not a butterfly kiss, all soft and feathery, but a real kiss that makes my head feel dizzy and light. I can't bear the idea of leaving her, though I'm desperate to go home.

I'm thinking about kissing Raven again when the nurse enters the room. Dad's here, she announces. Instantly, my head is a jumble of questions. I want to know everything, like why he left us and what he's been doing for the last five years. Does he have another wife? Another family? I used to think that I saw him everywhere, driving his silver Pontiac through the streets of Eastview. I used to hate him for leaving us the way he did. But I don't feel that way so much any more. I'm not angry, really. All I want is for him to be part of our lives again.

My stomach tightens when I think of actually seeing him. I'm terrified and excited at the same time. I wonder what The Duke would do in a situation like this, but I can't think of a single thing. I am feeling as though my head is going to burst . . . when a man appears in the doorway.

In an instant, all the questions and words abandon me, and the years of imagined conversations vanish like ghosts in the air. I feel so small, like the kid I was when he left. What do you say after five years of silence? How do you fill the gap created by so much time?

I turn to him and he's looking back at me with eyes that are just like mine. He smiles, and I feel the time slip away between us—all the anger and sorrow and emptiness. It washes away, like tears in the rain. Something flutters in its place, as gentle and promising as Raven's kiss. I know that nothing can ever be the same. I know that we can never be a family again, the way we once were.

But things will be better now, I'm sure of it. They just have to be.

Corn Dodgers

Corn dodgers, also known as johnnycakes or journey cakes (presumably because they were taken on long journeys) were a mainstay in pioneer cooking, along with beans and coffee. Dodgers were simple and very cheap to make, and the cornmeal was easy to transport, with a long shelf life. There are as many recipes for these little cakes as there are cooks.

2 cups yellow cornmeal
1 teaspoon salt
2 teaspoons butter or shortening
1¾ cups boiling water

Mix the cornmeal and salt. Work the butter in with your fingers or a pastry cutter. Pour the boiling water over the dry ingredients, stirring until smooth. Grease a heavy, 12-inch frying pan (preferably cast iron). Set over medium-low heat. Drop teaspoonfuls of the batter onto the pan. Cook until golden, about five minutes each side. Serve the cakes hot with butter and maple syrup or jelly. Makes 12–15 cakes.

Acknowledgments

Sincerest thanks to my editor and good friend, Lynne Missen, and the entire crew at HarperCollins. Special thanks to Kenneth Oppel and Janice Kulyk Keefer for their kindness, and to Sophie Tupholme for providing invaluable feedback on the manuscript. Thanks to all my friends for their support and caring, especially George and Eva, Doug and Naomi, Carol Shaw Peirson, Michio Takagi, the Dixits, Akka, Chris and Richard, Dom, Cath, and the Moles: Marie, Laura and Steve. Big thanks to Vicki, Gus, Gussie, Eliza and Jeannie for the wonderful honeymoon escape. And most of all, profound thanks to my entire family for everything, Mum, Mark, Jasmine, Rita, Cindy, Norman, Cassel, Hayden, Monika, Michael, Mike, Sean, Nick, Charlene, Jim, Aunt Giovanna, and especially Brian and Wesley, my love, my light, my life.